NARCISSISTIC REFLECTIONS

by Victor Peters

Order this book online at www.trafford.com
or email orders@trafford.com

Most Trafford titles are also available at major online book retailers.

Printed in Victoria, BC, Canada.

ISBN: 978-1-4269-0150-8 (sc)

*Our mission is to efficiently provide the world's finest, most comprehensive book publishing
service, enabling every author to experience success. To find out how to publish your book,
your way, and have it available worldwide, visit us online at www.trafford.com*

Trafford rev. 2/17/2010

 www.trafford.com

North America & international
toll-free: 1 888 232 4444 (USA & Canada)
phone: 250 383 6864 ♦ fax: 812 355 4082

Dedications

I WOULD LIKE to dedicate this meager epistle to Lawrie's parents Jimmy and Chrissy Kergan and to Frank and Phyllis Peters, my parent's, to whom we owe more than we can ever repay.

Jimmy and Chrissy Kergan   Frank and Phyllis Peters

Preface

I DECIDED TO write these memoirs of my teaching career and associated exploits for my children and grandchildren and other generation that may follow. Although the exploits may not be overly exciting, I have tried to keep them as accurate as memory permits. The main purpose is to give some insight into what life and schools were like way back in my day.

It is also designed to help them realize that their occupation is not just an occupation but also a window to the world. It can, if taken advantage of, offer opportunities for them to investigate their world. Through this investigation they will become more tolerant of others and so influence others to do the same, bringing about a more just and socially conscious world. These are ideals that may never come to pass but if we do not strive towards them we can only bring the world to an undesirable end.

The destruction of the world by man is not the inevitable end if we strive hard to prevent it and so the world may endure until nature herself decided to ring down the final curtain.

Chapter 1

WHAT PLANTED THE SEED TO BECOME A TEACHER?

---

*What springs forth from the seed
is determined by the conditions.*

A TEACHER! How could I be a teacher, I was never what one could normally call a student. I can only imagine the laughter that would have resulted, if ever my teachers had discussed my becoming a member of their honorable profession. As a student I managed to pass my courses with average marks and as little work as possible. The best mark I ever made was in Health Nine, the result of a clerical error. One of my best friends, named Ernie Patterson preceded me alphabetically on the marks list and this resulted in Ernie getting a C and me receiving his A. Beside the "brilliant" student with which my teachers had to cope, they also had to tolerate an overgrown, skinny six footer, dressed in a plaid wool shirt, complete with a package of Export A cigarettes, blue jeans and lumberjack Kodiak boots, all at the grand age of thirteen. Such behavior was not designed to show disrespect to my teachers but rather to develop a Wild West cowboy/lumberjack image.

Mr. Henry Jay, Headmaster of Holmwood
School, Surrey England. A man who taught
me more than he ever suspected.

Junior high and high school continued in this vain,
guaranteeing that I would not be the valedictorian of my
graduating class. Despite the effect this obviously negative
behavior must have had on my instructors, they in turn had
a fairly positive influence on me. All the teachers I had, in
one way or another, had some affect on me choosing to be a
teacher, some having a much greater influence than others,
although at the time, neither they nor I knew it. One such
person was my headmaster in England. This kindly, yet
strict man was Mr. Henry Jay. He had a knack of handling
children so as to command the greatest respect and exact a
high level of obedience. He would have never allowed the
behavior I exhibited in the Canadian school, image or no
image. Yet he did everything in his power to stimulate the
spirit of adventure and self worth by introducing us to the
works of Rudyard Kipling, Charles Dickens, Mark Twain
and many more. He always impressed upon us the glory
of the British Empire and the fact that failure was not an

acceptable form of behavior. Perhaps this had something to do with the fact that we were in the midst of World War Two.

I was eleven when my family moved to Canada as a result of my older sister's emigration the previous year to marry Lawrence Cotter, her Canadian soldier fiancé. In Canada I encountered a teacher named Mr. Carlson. Although his success in teaching me the fundamentals of English were somewhat limited, which was no fault of his, he did continue to stimulate my interest in geography and history, now known as social studies. Beside this discipline, he taught me that sometimes-drastic action was necessary to accomplish what you wished to achieve.

It was late May and the weather had been very warm. The old storm windows were those removed every spring and added every fall. This particular year the windows had failed to be removed despite many requests by staff to do so. Walking into the room one afternoon, Mr. Carlson encountered a room temperature of eighty degrees Fahrenheit. Something snapped! Taking a baseball bat, he proceeded to smash out all the lower panes from one end of the room to the other. Everyone in the room sat in dead silence, mouth-hanging open, aghast at the fact that this normally sane man had turned into a total mental case. No disciplinary infractions occurred during that class period. The action produced results. Next day the storm windows were off and the inner windows repaired, a lesson to reinforce the old adage that actions speak louder than words.

Three high school teachers played a role in influencing my future. The first was Miss Farmer who taught an option in music appreciation, a course I was forced to take in order to obtain enough credits for my grade ten year. She must have shuddered when she looked over her class and spotted this overgrown lumberjack sitting at the back, lounging like a long piece of kelp floating in a tidal pool. Most of the class, as was the case with a great many optional subjects, contained other musical amoeba like myself. She ploughed on, introducing the classics and managing to make us listen to the intricacies of great music. Somehow she made

The long piece of kelp that sat at the back of the room

classical music interesting and intriguing, at least to me and I believe others. At sixteen I bought my first classical recording, Gaite Parisienne by Offenbach, the first of many classical selections in my collection. I doubt if she ever knew she had such a huge influence on that gangly piece of kelp. What a shame she never got to know!

The second teacher, also a lady, by the name of Miss Dorothy McNary struck a chord in my subconscious. She taught English and English literature, a subject with which, as previously mentioned, I had little interest. She was a determined lady and took no guff from the big teenage boys in her class. We nicknamed her 'swivel hips' because of her sergeant major stride. Although I passed her courses I never came near making the honor role, no fault of hers. She did impress me with her fairness and consistent treatment of the students in her class, she was also a good teacher needless to say.

Mr. Pitt, principal of Claresholm High School.
He was a man with a social conscience.
He exhibited it, he didn't preach it.

The final member of the group was Mr. Pitt, who was not only our math and physics teacher but also principal of the Claresholm High School. All students in the school, I am sure, had a great deal of respect for this gentleman. He exemplified the morals and ethics one would like to instill in ones own children and they in theirs. He was a teacher who had a thorough understanding of the subject matter he taught, a quality absolutely necessary in this profession and one I tried hard to duplicate when I became a teacher, although did not always attain. He was also very wise in the ways one should try to develop life skills. He was the first to make me think about the great things my parents did for me, at a time in my life when all developing teens get the idea that they know everything and their parents are totally devoid of any common sense. He could relate stories (probably from experience with thousands of teens that had passed through his care) illustrating and reinforcing in my mind that parents made decisions for you and gave advice to you not from ignorance but from the valuable teacher known as experience. He certainly made me think, even if I still continued to ignore both his and my parent's efforts, only to realize years later how wise both he and my parents really were. On the whole, I liked most of the teachers I encountered during my school years, even though I am sure that the feeling wasn't totally mutual. In my own weird make up I was impressed by the ability of these people to have, in most cases, an influence for good on young people. Thus this could well have been one aspect that led me to make my choice.

For fear that I create the impression that I chose my profession solely because of the high standards of others I encountered, let me set the situation straight. As stated, my marks were adequate but never outstanding. As a result I never received my matriculation at the end of grade twelve. Math, chemistry and French had fallen short of the fifty per cent mark. Why I didn't take biology, the main area I went on to study, instead of chemistry I will never know. French at that time was a compulsory subject and so I had no choice but to take it.

In the fifties the student population, the result of the baby boom era, resulted in a great shortage of teachers. Therefore, the government of the day had to introduce a program known as Junior E, which was a one year program designed to fill the need in the classroom for teachers at the elementary and junior high levels. It proved to be my opportunity to get a foot in the door of the profession that had been germinating in my mind. Also my good friend Ernie Patterson, from whom I had stolen the health mark, had also fallen short of his matriculation requirements. He too was contemplating a career in education. Thus in September of nineteen fifty-six, he and I enrolled in the Junior E program at the University of Alberta.

Chapter 2

UNIVERSITY AND ITS EFFECTS.

Not all knowledge is drawn from the same well.

M Y JUNIOR E year of university was to me a great disappointment. Perhaps it was the program and the fact so much needed to be covered in such a short time. I can't fault most of the instructors although some seemed to be totally ignorant of what life in a real school was like. However, in the majority they were good instructors, in that they had paid their dues to get where they were. They were not just book taught as many instructors are today, having never seen the inside of a public school classroom. Thus many teachers as a result and in my opinion, go into the classroom unprepared for what it is really like. All the psychological studies about student behavior and what it is actually like are often a universe apart. As one bright individual said, "If psychologists ever get an understanding of human behavior, their knowledge will be invaluable." From my own experience with many of these learned persons, the comment contains a great deal of truth. However, I digress.

My instructors in the main had all taught school, some in a one-room schoolhouse. Many had experience as school administrators, as well as school superintendents, in the days when superintendents had their finger on the pulse of the schools in their jurisdiction, and then they had become instructors of others who wished to follow in their footsteps. Despite all this practical instruction, I found the whole situation a rather dissatisfying experience. The fact that we had to take thirteen courses in one year as opposed to the regular university student's five, and that we were perceived by other students on campus to be a rather inferior group, didn't help. This latter of course had foundation in that they had worked hard and achieved their matriculation standing, while many of us had not. Yet another factor may have been that "Mr. Brilliance" had never really learned to apply himself in the field of academics.

As we were expected to be able to teach all subjects at the elementary and junior high levels it was necessary to take courses in art and music. Art, I thought would be to my liking as I believed I had a little talent in this area. The instructor was obviously an advocate of abstractionism and even if he wasn't, he seemed abstract to me. I, on the other hand, was more of a realist, something I still pride myself in being. This all came to a head in one art class where we were given a piece of clay and asked to produce some artistic masterpiece. I diligently worked away, producing a rather good likeness of a wee Scotty dog. I was so pleased with myself that I dubbed the piece "Jock' a very unique and ingenious title I thought. It was here that the instructor and I parted company on what he and I considered art. He turned Jock around in his hand several times and then plunked it back on the desk, shortening Jock's stature by a good half inch and announced it warranted a C. I was extremely deflated by the gesture and the mark and, having always been a shy and retiring fellow, made up my mind that the man was an idiot. This concept was reinforced when he turned to the desk next to me, looked at the magnificent spherical ball of clay produced by a fellow classmate and handling it as though it had just been produced by Michelangelo, placed it carefully on the desk and gave the fellow an A. Do I hold grudges? You damn rights I do, for I still haven' t forgotten, even though it was fifty or more years ago. This instructor obviously never taught me to appreciate the simple and artistic things in life, for to this day I cannot imagine why the National Art Gallery would pay some two million dollars for two blue stripes separated by a red one. Thus my inability to get the true feeling of what real art was all about, cost me a failing grade at the Christmas break.

Music was another course that presented problems to me and I readily admit this was due to my own stupidity. The music course required us to purchase and learn to play a recorder, a skill I never accomplished, even though my grandson subsequently learned to play it at the age of eight. This I feel was the result of me being unable to break out of my cowboy/lumberjack persona. It seemed to me that carrying this musical stick to class, by someone who had achieved the right to attend a university was beneath my dignity both as a man and a scholar, possibly both being open to question. Thus, having carried it once to class, trying hard to keep it concealed from the prying eyes of Joe-heavens-knows-who and who didn't give a tinkers curse anyway, forced me to place it in my bureau drawer, from whence it never saw the light of day again, until I packed my bags at the end of the year. Luckily there were other aspects to the course, which enabled me to obtain a passing grade in the long run, but by Christmas music was added to my list of subjects that I was failing.

As if this wasn't bad enough, psychology and health were presenting me with problems as well. This may well be one of the reasons, like the art course, that I have a low appreciation of psychologists. The instructor, a Dr.

Pilkington, a very practical man, could understand the problems I was having and magnanimously gave me a bare passing grade. Four years later when I went back to complete my degree, I found to my horror that the Department of Education had it recorded as a failing grade and that it appeared I was destined to repeat a course I dislike so vehemently. I immediately went to Dr Pilkington and explained that my transcript had shown it as a pass. To indicate how times have changed he immediately picked up the phone and called the Department of Education. After explaining the problem briefly to the person at the other end, the disembodied voice stated that it must have been a clerical error, to which Dr. Pilkington suggested the clerk involved should consider becoming a garbage collector and throw himself into his work. The problem was solved, the episode ingrained in my mind to this day. When I became a teacher and later an administrator, I always tried to solve students and teachers problems with the least amount of rigmarole possible.

In contrast to Dr. Pilkington was our health instructor. This gentleman, who will remain nameless, taught the health methods course, a course that would have made most persons assigned to teach it play truant from class. Our instructor seemed to enjoy it. His constant theme was the need to be prepared, a boy scout no doubt. At each lecture he would produce his box of recipe cards upon which his lectures were neatly typed. In a monotonous drone he would read off the information before him, while constantly reiterating the need for careful preparation. I have to agree the material was covered and definitely sequential. This process works but allows for no variation or deviation, a necessary ingredient which often leads to some exciting and thought provoking discussions, from my experience in the classroom.

Dependence on such a rigid system can lead to problems, as was demonstrated to us one day when in class this well orchestrated approach seemed to go dreadfully wrong. The lecture proceeded as usual when suddenly the topic changed in midstream. Surprise and panic registered on his round and now ruddy face. Cards were quickly scanned and placed in separate piles in a terrifying silence. Organization had taken wing and abandoned our organizational guru. Sequential cards found, the lecture proceeded only to be derailed again a few minutes later. So the lecture went until the period bell mercifully ended his dilemma. We found out later that a couple of fellows from the previous class had returned to the lecture room while the instructor was absent, noticed the card box and decided on an out of season Halloween trick. They shuffled the cards and returned them to the box. This did one thing to improve our lot, as from that day forward the preparation theme seemed to take a back seat to the lecture material. I suppose he did more to make us better teachers than he knew, as it taught us to develop flexibility in our own planning.

As mentioned, I did not find the program exciting or one that treated you as an adult but continued in the same vein as high school. This gave me the opportunity to make excuses for my own inadequacies to cope with this less than advanced educational situation. As a result I did not do well and at Christmas break, my marks in half the courses were less than adequate. Now many students made the deans list; I too made the list but not the honor list. I had a personal invitation from the dean to visit him for a one on one chat. The chat however seemed to be a little one sided and the message was very clear: shape up or ship out. As I was attending university on an extremely tight budget, the whole year costing me nine hundred and twenty dollars of hard earned money, I recalled Mr. Jay's message, that failure was not an acceptable situation, and decided to apply myself. The year finally came to a close and I managed to pass with average marks, but best of all, I was released from my year of academic misery. The saving grace was the many enjoyable and some rather unusual situations I encountered, situations one didn't find in small town rural Alberta. Also I could now look forward to employment that would give me a steady income of twenty four hundred dollars a year, with the Macleod School Division. Looking back on it I had never been so rich before or since.

Chapter 3

THE SIDE EFFECTS OF
GOING TO THE CITY

*You can take the boy out of the country, but you can't take
the country out of the boy. You can however warp him.*

AVING ALWAYS lived in a small community, going to
the city seemed an exciting experience. My friends
Ernie Patterson and Harold Loney, who unlike Ernie
and I had achieved his matriculation and was entering pre-
law, had made arrangements to occupy a basement suite
in the home of a friend of my parents. This seemed like a
good arrangement as it was reasonable and on a direct bus
route to the university. However, no sooner had we settled
into our lodgings, than the City of Edmonton decided to
discontinue this route, which left us no alternative but to
take a circuitous route through downtown. This became
an intolerable situation causing us to move residence. We
finally located a boarding house only twenty blocks from
the university, an easy walk for students trying to save
money. Fortunately it was on a good bus route so when
the weather turned a little inclement and the wind chill
hit minus forty we could splurge and ride the bus to class

in comfort. So the three of us settled into the fourteen by fourteen-foot square room, two sharing a double bed and the lucky one a single

The landlady had an uncanny skill of keeping food cost to a minimum. When serving food she gave you a couple of ounces of meat, a spoonful of potatoes and two spoons of cooked frozen peas. The second spoonful was given a small shake and what managed to stay in the spoon was yours. Luckily she always placed a loaf of sliced bread on the table. Those who ate fast and had a long reach could snag three or four slices of bread to help fill the empty spaces in their stomachs.

As there were fourteen of us staying at the house, as well as the owner's family of four, there was an interesting assortment of individuals Four that were real characters were Leonard, the Morrisons and Agie. Agie was a German girl who lived with two other girls in a self-contained suite on the top floor. She had a sense of humor that kept all around her in constant laughter and good spirits. However, one of her most outstanding talents was her ability to throw accurately. One evening on the way back to the house from an evening out, she started throwing stones at lampposts. From fifty feet away her rock hit the pole square on the money. The boys in the group, not to be outdone decided to show off their skills. All missed. Agie again took aim and again hit the pole dead center. A volley of rocks from all present sailed through the air and just from sheer numbers one or two made contact. Agie's third rock just sailed by but was close enough to make the pole duck. Her next few rocks made contact. At this point we conceded she was number one and dubbed her dead eyed dick. Unfortunately the girls moved out of the house a month later, but was fortunate from the point of view it left the suite vacant, a chance we jumped at to escape our two hundred square foot prison.

The Morrisons were a young English couple. He was looking for work and was away all day and her interests wandered to another fellow in the house, which led to some loud confrontations between her and her husband. Coming from the country and having worked on a farm, I thought I had heard all the swear words going, but obviously not. I didn't realize that amount of profanity born from sexuality existed. My vocabulary expanded immensely but the volume of the instruction made it difficult to concentrate on one's academic endeavors. Suffice to say the marriage didn't last and they left our tranquil domicile

Leonard was a permanent resident; he had been there as long as the owners or perhaps longer. He was an electrician and had to get up early for work, something he found very difficult. The landlady, as a special service to Leonard, would give him a wake up call. She would pound on the door and shout, "Leonard, hit the floor".

To which Leonard would reply with a mumbled, "yea."

"Let's hear you hit the floor", she would shout.

Leonard would lift his boot an inch or so off the floor and let it drop.

"Now the other shoe Leonard". He would repeat the operation, "Get up or I'm coming in, I know your game", she would rattle the door handle and Leonard would hit the floor. This game was repeated Monday through Friday, with holidays the exception. One of the reasons Leonard had trouble getting up was his addiction to brandy. He would pour brandy into a water glass with the comment five fingers in the bottom of a rain barrel. He was generous and liked to have a drinking buddy, so if the academics weren't going well or weren't too pressing, a visit to Leonard's room was a good tension reliever

One evening Leonard suggested we should go to a movie, so we jumped in his van, he already having had several brandies, and we proceeded to the other side of the city. During the movie Leonard fell asleep and upon awakening at the end, he stood, staggered into the isle and then backwards against the flow of the crowd but in response to the law of gravity. He ran into a hail of abuse and profanity but continued to act like a breakwater stemming the flow of the tide. We were finally able to get behind him and push him up and out of the theater. Once outside I suggested I should drive but Leonard in a slurred voice assured us he could drive and besides that he had the keys. He staggered around the van, tried opening the door; but he couldn't because his full weight was leaning against it. This brought about a great deal of cursing and mumbling. He finally rolled to one side and the door sprang open, almost throwing him to the ground. He slid in under the steering wheel, groped and swore trying to find the ignition and finally succeeded in bringing the van motor to life. We had piled in by this time, obviously not happy with the situation and certainly not making the most sensible choice, but we too had indulged in a few brandies, despite the fact we were under age

Driving back across the city we felt our way back along the Groat Road. The front bumper showering sparks from the high curb, as we made contact every hundred yards or so. I am sure this wasn't the first time Leonard had driven home using the Braille method. Once again back on the south side we wove our way down Eighty Second Avenue. All was going well until some individual decided to climb out of his car; I think he must have been drunk as well; we were heading right for him when I had the presence of mind to grab the steering wheel, and we missed him by inches. We made it home with a slightly more sober driver.

Once the girls had vacated the upstairs suite we moved up, thinking that cooking our own food plus more room would be a definite plus. It was. We acquired a fourth person named Gerald Weibe. He asked us if he could join us, as he found it difficult to work in the room he shared with another individual, who often brought his girl friend up for a quick romp in the hay. So the four of us settled in and soon became an efficient crew, dividing up and carrying out the household chores.

Our common bathroom was on the second floor. One morning, being the first up, I went down to get showered. As I hit the second floor landing I was surprised to find large red footprints much like ones found in a mall to direct you to the public washrooms. This was different, I thought, and continued into the bathroom to be greeted by what looked like a murder scene. So used had we become to the unusual that no feeling of panic occurred but simply more a feeling of annoyance that some inconsiderate soul had buggered up the bathroom. After showering I washed out the sink, brushed my teeth and went back upstairs and told the others what they may encounter. We later found out that Frank, a newcomer, had come home drunk and had fallen down the stairs as he was attempting to head for the bathroom. Cutting his head open on the banister as he fell and bleeding profusely, he regained his balance and staggered back, this time gaining the bathroom. He obviously completed his task and, still bleeding, made his way downstairs to his room, where he remained ensconced for several days until he reappeared with his black eye and badly gashed forehead. It would appear that, had he died, no one would have become concerned until he started to smell.

Although the academic year was not to my liking or as I had expected it to be, my non-academic year certainly proved to be a lot more interesting. So in retrospect I can only conclude I got one hell of an education that year, all of which probably helped me, if not to become a better teacher, at least one with a lot better understanding of life.

Chapter 4

MY FOUR YEARS IN CLARESHOLM

I came, I saw and I attempted teaching.

SCHOOL DAYS, school days, good old golden rule days had come at last. After working that summer as a farm laborer, I was now going to enter a white-collar profession. September third, nineteen fifty-seven was a day etched in my mind forever. The day was a beautiful fall southern Alberta day, the air crisp and invigorating. I walked to school, as I had not achieved enough wealth at this point to purchase a car. Carrying my carefully scripted lesson plans in my briefcase, I was sure my health professor would have been proud. I strode along the sidewalk feeling an inner pride, a pride derived from the fact that I had shed the bonds of my working class background. I had been the first in our immediate family to enter a learning institution beyond the public school level and one of the few in the whole Peters clan to do so, not that my siblings really had the opportunity presented to them.

Front View of Claresholm Elementary
School, build around 1954

As king of the world I entered my school, a new building of only a few years and my own classroom, which the previous week I had spent time trying to make inviting and exciting. I lay my plans on the desk and stacked the books I would need for the day neatly on one corner of my desk. This was the way I always started something new but it seldom survived much past the first week. Eying the scene with satisfaction, I turned my attention to writing in my very best hand on the shiny new green, blackboard "Good morning class, my name is Mr. Peters." It surprises me how at the time I felt ecstatic at having my name in lights so to speak. I felt so original, failing to realize, the phrase, "Good-morning-class-my-name-is", was being written on thousands of blackboards, or green boards as the case may be, all over the country. Waiting in anticipation of my first class I busied myself making sure all my posters and other paraphernalia were in order. This was my ship and I was her captain, all I needed now was the crew. The bell rang and the supervising playground teacher lined the kids up by grade and in they marched. An excited yet quiet chatter announced their approach and the thirty or so kids swarmed into the room

Back view of Claresholm Elementary,
my classroom top left corner

"Find a seat", I instructed, with a commanding voice and one I hoped carried the appropriate amount of authority. At this point I had no formal seating plan. That would come later. This grade six class had now reached the age of sexual segregation and the girls made a move for the front and window side of the room and the boys to the back and nearer to the exit door. I called the group to order and the room fell silent, obviously the result of seasoned teachers' training from the years before. One thing definitely hadn't changed: the big farm boys with plaid shirts and boots, but no cigarettes, sat in the back corner closest to the door. I formed an immediate bond with these kids but I made up my mind right then and there I wasn't going to take the type of attitude from them I had exhibited not so many years before.

We started, as all classes did in those days, with the Lord's Prayer, which was rattled off in a staccato monotone, lacking feeling and understanding, as I was to find out later. That completed, I now moved on to roll call placing a diagonal line across a square box in the register. This divided the day into two parts. If a student was absent you placed an "a" in the appropriate section, none was absent that morning

Now came the time to put into action those months of boredom I had survived the year before. Each lesson went well, with students bright, shiny and eager to please. The bright student's hands shot up to answer the questions I posed. What a piece of cake this is, I thought. Then I came to realize that the slow kid in the back was going to avoid answering any questions if I didn't push him-and it was usually a him-whereas the bright kids, more often than not girls, needed no encouragement to stand out. After several months, or was it years, I realized bright students hardly needed a teacher; they would achieve success without you. If you wanted to call yourself a teacher you had to encourage and help the person not answering the questions. I also realized that these students weren't actually stupid, though some did lack the mental capacity of many of their peers, but mainly they were extremely shy or insecure. These were the kids we often ignored because they didn't make us look good in the classroom when the superintendent came to call. These were the same students you needed to work with for they were the potential troublemakers, especially in junior high.

I get ahead of myself. The day went well and at the end, some students linger to ask a few questions about my likes or dislikes. I had taken psychology, they hadn't, but they were sizing me up for manipulation later. So the days passed and gradually the newness was wearing off and the students started doing things students did, chatter, shoot the odd spit wad, pass notes and the bright ones would try to throw you a curve and watch your reaction. As the lessons became less interesting my ability to motivate these young minds was becoming, to say the least, a challenge. Somehow all the knowledge I had learned, seemed to get used up in the first week or two. Now what? Well, the veterans didn't seem to have many problems, so I bottled my pride and sat down with a couple of them to seek some answers.

The first good advice I received was to arrange a class exchange in subjects in which you didn't feel competent, with a teacher more competent in the field. I immediately pawned off my music class, I guess I should have paid more attention in my music class but it was too late now. I managed to exchange my music for the physical education class of a lady teacher on staff, what a relief that was. The other good advice was making the little buggers work. Make sure you have plenty of extra things for those kids who do the work in ten minutes that it takes others all period to do. Unlike cattle, one couldn't just herd them all along the same well-trodden path. Gradually the fact these kids were individuals and not just a class of homogeneous robots became more and more obvious. Other good advice was, let the students enlarge on topics of interest to them that come up during your lesson. Dictatorial discipline I have few problems with, dictatorial instruction tends to develop non-thinking students. Talk with the kids who are having trouble and develop a good rapport with them. Looking back on it, these are things any idiot should know but surprisingly enough they are things you learn as you watch and listen to other teachers, or have battered home by experience as you spend time in a confined space with children and young adults. This is when you begin to realize that teaching is not just employment but an experience that broadens your own knowledge and, in the case of most teachers, develops a strong social conscience. This is also when you realize some people will succeed in society and do well, and others will always need assistance.

In those days all classroom teachers were supplied with a regulation strap. Although I know some people today are horrified at the thought of their child being the subject of corporal punishment, it certainly gave the teacher control. Days occurred when things didn't always go the way you expected or desired. Maybe it was a day when you were not right on top of the world or a day when the students were feeling restless. I am sure with the perfect behavior exhibited by students today and the wonderful psychological training teachers receive, bad days no longer occur. However, back in the fifties they did and a sharp reprimand didn't always bring things back to order. The act of opening one's desk drawer and placing the strap on the desk produced almost immediate results.

There were occasions when the strap was used and two memorable occasions come to mind. The one situation involved the son of the local Norwegian Lutheran Church minister. Daniel had been misbehaving in such a way that he was becoming a strain on the nerves. I finally decided it was time to take the bull by the horns. The next time he acted up I called him to the front and gave him a couple of good whacks on the hand. That evening after school I was in the playground laying out some baseball diamonds when, looking up, I saw Daniel's father appear around the corner of the school. Here comes "a suffering little children to come unto me" speech, I thought. He approached, greeting me with a broad smile. Immediately up went my guard.

"I hear you had to strap Daniel today", he said.

"Yes," I replied, "he was becoming a constant disturbance in class

"I see", he said, "I completely understand, he is behaving the same way around home. I concur with what you did, I should have done it myself months ago, and it was obviously long over due".

Daniel's attitude improved along with his marks. It shows what parent teacher cooperation can do in achieving results that actually benefit the child. Daniel not only became a model student but one of the best scholars in the class. I never realized until then that a little stress could sometimes cause a jump in I.Q; if not a jump at least an upsurge in the use of the gray matter with which we are endowed.

The other occasion involved about a dozen students some from my class and some from the other grade six. An area to the side of the school had been landscaped and seeded to grass. A general announcement was made over the intercom not to go on this area. That particular day I was the playground supervisor. Having circled the playground I came around the corner of the school to where the seeded area existed. To my amazement a group of students were playing tag in and about the forbidden zone. I gave out a drill sergeant bellow and everyone immediately froze. I commanded they line up in single file and I marched them down to the office. Lining them up facing me with a hand out I proceeded to give each one a whack on the outstretched hand. The grass grew undisturbed once word had spread through the school.

The real effect of this episode I didn't know until a few years later when they and I had advanced to grade eight. Being delayed by a few minutes getting to class I turned into the hall where my class was located. A couple of boys, who had been involved in the grass incident, were taking a late drink at the water fountain. When they heard me coming they scurried for the room. As they entered the room they gave the warning "look out! Here comes 'The Whip'." This was the nickname given me after the lawn incident, I found out years later at a school reunion when we were swapping stories about the good old days. Reunions are great to attend as you get a chance to meet your students as mature adults. As you are no longer the authority figure, they are willing to discuss freely and without fear of reprisal, the days you were their teacher. From our conversations I was pleased to find they generally found me fair and easy to approach. That wouldn't be a bad epitaph. It isn't a glowing endorsement of my teaching but I value it as a personal endorsement. It was teachers with similar characteristics that I found made an impression me.

I guess the pressures can get to you after you have spent three years in the classroom or maybe sometimes just stupid things happen. I remember the day I was doing my best to implant some science information in the minds of my grade eight class, when there came a knock at my classroom door. Through the glass panel in the door I could see Mr. Runquist, a colleague. I stopped whatever I was doing marched to the door and preceded, like I was in my right mind, to knock on the inside. The class went deadly silent, something that probably wouldn't happen today. They all stared with a look of incredulity on their faces, which basically said, we often suspected it but now we know for sure, he is finally ready for the rubber room.

Realizing what I had done I burst into laughter, opened the door and said to Mr. Runquist, "come on in. You see what these people drive you to." I hopped across the room gesturing like a crazy man. The students, now regaining their composure, roared with laughter at the stupidity of their teacher. Mr. Runquist gave them a sound reprimand, in jest, for causing such mental stress in their teacher who was trying so hard to instill a little science into their devious minds.

It is very important, I feel, that a teacher be in control, but also empathetic with the students, it will make control much easier and teaching possible. I have encountered a few colleagues, who had lost their control and when this happens the students will tend to take the control from you, the result is nothing but chaos. If you have control your instructional period will be productive, resulting in less need to impose a great deal of homework, something that should definitely be minimal in elementary school. Junior high is early enough to start establishing a regimented homework schedule. Elementary school years are the years for students to interact with ones peers in games and playtime, to learn the socialization skills some seem to be lacking today This possibly could be the reason more bullying and like activities are occurring at higher grade levels. As I now sit back and see my grandchildren, at this point, one in grade four and the other in grade two and observe the massive amount of homework they are assigned, I shudder. I have concerns that either we are expecting too much academically or not enough actual teaching is going on in class time. Maybe we are becoming more concerned with quantity than quality. From my experience the fact a student hasn't acquired a specific quantity of knowledge is not as important as knowing how to accumulate quality knowledge.

When I taught science it was more important to be able to develop the apparatus to test what you hoped to find out than to use store bought apparatus that would more or less guarantee the results. worse yet is having the teacher demonstrate the experiment while the students just watch. Half the challenge is setting up the procedure. This is one reason why children do not need all their toys to be manufactured by others but rather they should invent some by themselves using their own imaginations. The need to develop curiosity is extremely important in our learning process. The idea that curiosity is important was brought home to me by one of my grade six students. I came into the room to find this young lady looking through some papers on my desk. I asked her, "What are you doing"?

She said, "I was curious to see what mark I received on my assignment".

"I see", I replied. "Are you not aware of the old quotation about curiosity killing the cat.

"Oh yes", she said, "but satisfaction brought him back".

I had never heard the latter part of that quote but it gave me food for thought. If I could create curiosity followed by satisfaction then possibly I might have a great teaching tool. If we learn the ability to attack problems, even if at first we don't succeed, we will with time find the solution and lick the problem. Presenting the child with workbooks and prescribed pathways only opens up the door to persons or groups that wish to have us follow them without any critical thinking or analysis. Whether my thought on this matter is right or wrong, what is important is that a teacher must always be open to ideas regardless of the source. In looking back, that young girl in that one situation did more to make me a better teacher than many of the professionals I encountered in my career. It is the uncluttered mind of young children that makes teaching and working with students such a pleasure.

Continuing to digress in the philosophical vein, I believe it is unfortunate that we have taken teachers, in most cases very dedicated teachers, and reduced them to a tool responsible for teaching a direct, delineated and detailed curriculum set by experts. Expert being defined as follows: "ex" being a has-been and "spurt", being a drip under pressure. For fear of not completing the outlined tasks, teachers forgo much of their own creativity that induces pleasure and satisfaction into the act of teaching. This became evident to me when I spent five years teaching in Africa with The Canadian International Development Agency, where we as teachers had a great deal of freedom. Firstly, there was little or no parent involvement at the high school level. Secondly, we chose our own textbooks for the course and thirdly with limited equipment both teachers and students were very resourceful. The curriculum was a very basic outline that the teacher had to flesh out and because these same students were competing with students in many other countries in the world, the material had to be covered. It made one feel very professional and responsible to the students one was servicing. I will deal with this in more detail on the chapter dealing with the five years I spent in Uganda.

I concluded my four years in Claresholm having taught two years in grade six and two years in junior high. I left, having achieved my matriculation, to complete my Baccalaureate in Education. For those who experience a situation that takes ages to complete and what may take on an air of what seems like a never ending story, I wrote my French 30 exam six times before I achieved my fifty per cent pass mark. You would think with all that practice I would be able to parle le Francais, or become a UN interpreter, but no. However, I headed back to the University of Alberta, much less naive than the first time I entered it's halls of learning.

Chapter 5

MY RETURN TO THE
UNIVERSITY OF ALBERTA

Another attempt to draw water from the well.

I DECIDED THAT I would major in biological sciences and minor in physical education. The first stumbling block was, as I mentioned earlier in this discourse, the fact that the university was not aware I had passed my Junior E 101 psychology course. The next was that my science courses worked well but because of quarter courses, the physical education courses didn't. Also the fact I was expected to do two more sessions of practice teaching was going to prevent me from completing my degree in three years as I had planned. Changing to a physical science minor helped but practice teaching was going to mean another half year, something that was going to put a greater financial burden on me than I really wanted. As I now had an old car, I wasn't anxious to give it up to extend my stay in the hallowed halls of learning. Dr. Pilkington was still the assistant dean and so I made an appointment to see him and discuss my problem. He remembered me from two weeks earlier when the mark problem had cropped up with psychology. I was thinking he was going to be fed up with this young man with problems. He greeted me in a warm and friendly manner.

" Problems with psychology?" he said.

"No," I laughed. "I think all those problems are behind me". I went on to explain the dilemma with the practice teaching

He, in his same practical and logical fashion asked, "How long have you taught?"

"Four years", I said.

"Did you have satisfactory inspector's reports during that time"? He enquired

I was pleased to inform him that I had above average reports and that I would be more than happy to produce them.

"No need. If your reports were good, it seems redundant to spend time here doing what you already seem to know. I think it would be more advantageous for you to get back into the classroom at the earliest opportunity", he said. "Therefore we will indicate on your record that your teaching experience is sufficient to consider that part of the training completed"

God what a man, a paragon of wisdom and practicality! After those first few weeks of indecision and uncertainty I now embarked on a true university life. All those years of being a mediocre student were gone, I finally applied myself and discovered two things I was never sure about before. One: I could study and do well academically and two, (he said bragging modestly) I was a lot smarter than I thought. To that time I never considered myself capable of holding my own with others I thought were far more intelligent, but now my feeling of academic inferiority was drastically diminished. I no longer needed my world as a cowboy/lumberjack to give me a feeling of worth. This became even more evident to me when, in my first major zoology examination, I scored ninety four per cent and placed in the top ten percent of a class of six hundred students. Although my education courses were not as kind to me, mainly because I didn't find them as interesting as my science courses, I still did reasonably well. This again contained a lesson I tried to carry into the classroom; being well informed isn't enough, it is absolutely imperative to try and make instruction as exciting and interesting as possible. Although I tried hard, it was a situation that proved to be easier said than done. Very few have the knack to achieve this on a constant basis. One such person that comes to mind was Tommy Douglas. This man made political speeches so interesting and poignant, that to my knowledge he was the only politician who could fill a hall of any size not only with his own supporters but also with hundreds who held to the opposite end of the political spectrum. I recall hearing a true blue Tory saying he disliked the man immensely but I would travel fifty miles to hear him speak. Why? Because you could listen with interest and enjoyment about what he had to say.

The three years I spent finishing my degree were normal years, nothing too out of the ordinary happened. Each summer I would spend working to make sure I could eat during the next term. Between my third and forth year I landed a position with the Alberta Liquor Control Board, working in one of their liquor stores, which was fantastic for two reasons: the first was it grew into an evening shift during the winter session and two it increased my income. This was ideal as it worked well into my academic schedule and when I had exams the other employees would allow me to go to the beer room. Here I could study, only occasionally being disturbed to throw down a few more cases to replenish the stores supply. An added bonus to all this was the meeting of Harry Hill whom, having worked at the same liquor store the year before, had returned for a second.

Harry was also taking education, was married and had two children with another on the way. Harry had for several years been a traveling salesman for Engineered Homes but he and his wife Mary had decided he needed a more stable stay at home position. As a result Harry was majoring in music, an area in which he was very proficient, Mary was a laboratory technician and worked to keep food on the table and put Harry through university. During that year, Mary and Harry became my very good friends and I also became acquainted with Mary's father and mother, Jimmy and Chrissie Kergan, of Drumheller. I also found out that Mary had a brother and sister. The sister, Lawrie, was traveling the world and was in New Zealand working as a journalist. This didn't have much of an impact on my life at that point but at my graduation I met Lawrie who had returned home and was visiting the Hills at that time. To cut a long story short I dated Lawrie, as she was now working at the Calgary Herald and I had found a teaching position in High River, thirty five miles to the south of the city. The rest as they say is history. Two years later we were married.

Chapter 6

HIGH RIVER

Home to the hills

HIGH RIVER, one of the prettiest towns in Alberta, is situated at the edge of the rolling foothills of the Rocky Mountains and on the banks of the Highwood River. It was here I obtained my first high school teaching assignment. The principal was Mr. Floyd Henheffer, an excellent administrator who held the respect of both teachers and students alike. He was a strong disciplinarian who expected good behavior from the student body and a high standard of conduct from his staff. He achieved both and the result was a very well run school. It is surprising how this impacted on the high academic standards of the school. I realized years after how easy this made your teaching assignment and your ability to impart knowledge to the students in your charge. The actual disciplining that was necessary by the teacher was reduced to very little or none. In most cases, mainly because of peer pressure, few students failed to complete assignments on time, nor did they create problems in class. As a new teacher dealing with students of this age group in this environment, the reduced pressure on me that was the result, caused me to be extremely lucky, for I know of others who failed to stay in the profession because constant disciplining and poor behavior of the students made teaching too stressful. So it is that a good solid captain at the helm makes for smooth sailing and on the whole, a happier group of people; staff, students and parents.

Possibly in the early sixties, particularly in rural areas where I did all of my teaching, there existed a close relationship among school board, superintendent and principal. This in turn gave the principal a major role in choosing the staff with which he was going to work. It gave the principal a great deal of input into the general operation of the school division or county as the case may be. This also meant that the staff had a direct line through their principal to the governing body. Thus the whole system was one of interaction rather than a one way flow downward as it had a tendency to do twenty or so years later. The educational system was in evolution at this time and, probably because I was introduced into teaching at this juncture, I felt it was the best of times. When I became a principal, I tried to maintain this atmosphere of control without total dictatorship. As an example, the previous principal to Mr. Henheffer was known to stroll down town after ten o' clock on a school night and any student he encountered, he would send scurrying home. Can you imagine that scene today if the local school principal were to take on this role?

I realize I am generalizing when I say there was more cooperation between parents and teachers then, than exists today with all the parent committees and advisory boards. It seems we have taken simplicity and discarded it for complexity. This fact results in more people at the administrative end and proportionally less at the action end. I will say that we probably now have far better trained and, for a short time, more enthusiastic teachers than we have ever had. Unfortunately with the conflict between governments at all levels and over-zealous parent groups, often with hidden agendas, we find many frustrated persons in the classroom. This is editorializing but with a great deal of underlying truth, if what I hear many present-day teachers saying about their situation is accurate.

The front entrance to High River High School

My role in High River was mainly in the biological science area. We had a fine laboratory classroom with my office and animal room at one end. I raised rats, frogs and fruit flies for use in laboratory instruction. Just to add to the interest level in the room I had among other things a couple of garter snakes. Unfortunately the shelf on which the terrarium was sitting was not as strong as it appeared and one evening it crashed to the floor allowing the snakes to escape. I was out of town that evening and a fellow teacher, Corky Rousseau, who taught physical education and some junior science, received a frantic phone call from the janitor, a gentleman from Scandinavia

"Hey Corky, you better get up here to da school! Doze gosh darn snakes have escaped dare cage and are creeping up and down the darn hallway here. You can bet your sweet ass I'm not going to touch doze slimy buggars. You tell Peters to keep doze buggars in a better cage they can't get out of".

Corky corralled those sneaky critters and secured them for the evening. A little carpentry work made sure their new home would stay put

Laboratory block at High River High School

I had, believe it or not, been assigned to teach an option in psychology for a group of students like those who had taken Miss Farmers music appreciation course. To try and make it a more hands on experience I decided to deal with a section on learning behavior by having the students build a maze and attempt to teach rats to take the shortest route to a food source. During this session I received an inspection by a provincial high school inspector, a position that has gone the way of the dodo. A visit by such an individual was always a rectal sphincter-contracting situation, however the complexity of the apparatus and the enthusiasm of the students earned high praise from the inspector and led to a glowing report. Sometimes the gods do smile on you.

The class was taught in the old home economics room, as home economics was no longer being offered. However the electric stoves and other equipment were still in place and during one of the rat running sessions a rat escaped the maze and somehow managed to find its way into one of the stoves. As I have previously mentioned, a little digression from the subject area can also be a learning experience. Rounding up a few tools we started dismantling the stove. As we removed one panel the rat would move into another section of the stove. Gradually the stove became a mass of elements, panels and other miscellaneous bits and pieces. We finally capture the elusive rascal and confined it to quarters. Now came a real learning experience, putting the stove back together. The one thing I can say about people from rural areas is that they generally have an almost innate sense about machines and animals. Certainly the group had no trouble reassembling the stove and no one was any the wiser about the event

One other event that sticks in my mind with this same group, a situation of which I could hardly be proud or wished to be repeated, occurred during the last period of the day. The evening before I had gone into Calgary to visit Lawrie, something usually reserved for the weekend. We had gone to some special event, possibly something she was covering for the newspaper. Being very much in love we didn't want the evening to end and I stayed much later than I intended and I didn't leave until the early hours of the morning. Driving home I fell asleep at the wheel, something I have not done before or since. Luckily the car seemed to know its way home and I had covered a half-mile before I woke up and regained control.

Next morning I was up bright and early for school but by the end of the day I was feeling the effects of sleep deprivation. Putting the last few notes on the board for the class to copy, I felt myself falling sideways. Catching myself I realized my last word had trailed off into a long line arching three feet across the blackboard. The students thought I was having a heart attack or a fainting spell, but not what it turned out to be, a short power nap. I finished the note and sat down at my desk. The pleasant relief of a period bell fortunately brought the day to an end

The staff at the High River School was a very congenial group. Martha Houston, an older unmarried lady teacher pushing or past retirement age, something not uncommon in those day, taught English and English literature. She was an extremely well read person, not only in the areas of literature one associates rightly or wrongly with gray haired ladies, but in all areas. She was the type of person who, when she spoke you listened, for what she had to say was well worth hearing. She spoke with authority and you knew she could back up her information from many different sources; many more than the average well educated person could call upon. At one staff gathering the conversation somehow involved sex, child bearing and child rearing. Lawrie and I, who were now married but childless, and along with another couple in the same situation, plus Corky and Jeanette Rousseau, not childless and married for a number of years, along with Martha carried on a fairly lengthy discussion. Martha as always contributed, citing many sources to support her thesis. Her arguments to my recollection seemed sound; having experienced the last two as time went by. Later in the evening the wife of the other childless couple made the comment

"What would an old spinster like her know about the topic, she said chuckling, "she hasn't experienced any of those things.

I could guess that child bearing hadn't been an experience and I don't wish to comment on the first of the three areas. However, I would bet, experience or not, Martha was better informed than most in the group, including Corky and Jeanette. This may seem to shoot down the assertion I made about education professors who had not taught in a classroom were less qualified than those who had due to their inexperience in the real life situation. Their lectures revealed this lack of experience. In Martha's case, Lawrie and I agreed later having experienced all three, what she had to say was based on a solid foundation. It brings home the point, that experience is very helpful but a full investigation of all sides of a topic develops that illusive area we call wisdom

When I first moved to High River, Lawrie and I had met but were not a serious item and even prior to that I had thought of doing some traveling. I had made application to Jamaica and to the Canadian International Development Agency or C.I.D.A. The reply from Jamaica was not overly encouraging but the response from C.I.D.A was more enthusiastic, although at least a couple of years down the road. This seemed a good option as it would mean I could spent two years in High River in a well run school with good staff and students and a pleasant and friendly community

I had managed to rent the top floor of a large old house, which consisted of a two-bedroom apartment that was more than adequate for my needs. Also new on staff was the social studies teacher, Harvey Telford who was living in the hotel. He seemed like a nice quiet fellow and so at the end of September I invited him to share the apartment. Things went well for the first few weeks and in an attempt to introduce Harvey to a few friends of mine, we went to Claresholm to a party. In those days one did not party in the town where you taught, an advantage I suppose of teaching in the city. The evening was proceeding well until Harvey had a few too many beers. I had seen Dr. Jekyll and Mr. Hyde in the movies but I was about to experience it first hand. After too many drinks Harvey became loud and obnoxious and, like an old cow separated from her calf, was on the prod at the least provocation. It came to a climax when Harvey climbed on the coffee table and jumped on a few of the host records. The next thing I knew Harvey was being forcibly ejected from the house. At this point my brother Art, who was also at the party, luckily for me, decided it would be a good idea to take Harvey home. Harvey with a little not so gentle persuasion, was pushed out of the house and into my car and the three of us headed for High River

While on the drive home, a speeding car that had come out of some side road passed us, overtook a semi-trailer truck and disappeared. Shortly after the truck's brake lights came on and it screeched to a stop. We pulled up behind the truck and I got out to investigate. The car had missed the corner and rolled over several times, severely injuring the occupants. The trucker and I looked into the vehicle and he suggested I go and call an ambulance and the police. Luckily we were only a kilometer or two from Nanton. The ambulance and police called, we returned to the scene, and the emergency vehicles arrived within minutes. Harvey was now ready to fight everybody including the police so Art kept him under control with a bear hug and held him in the car. The injured occupants were removed and the truck and ourselves continued our travels. We arrived home and Harvey, still wanting to fight, provoked Art into landing a stiff blow on his torso, knocking him to the floor. Finally he became subdued and we put him to bed. My God, I thought, what have I got myself into, not to mention what would happen to our reputations if this ever got out into the community. It also showed that the need for teachers was still great for somehow Harvey had slipped through any screening process, although I will say he was certainly a very knowledgeable social studies teacher, even if he was a little unreliable. Did I say a little? However based on the student's performance at the end of the year he obviously imparted all the knowledge needed for the students to do well

One other incident (and it being only one more of many before Harvey and I parted company and I moved to Calgary), arose one morning. I walked out into the kitchen only to spy some large feet protruding into the center of the living room from the only armchair we had in the house. I peered in to find a large individual of native origin passed out awkwardly in the chair. I continued to the kitchen to prepare coffee and breakfast before getting ready for school. Shortly after, Harvey appeared on the scene

"Who is that in the living room"? He asked.

"Don't you know"? I answered, "You must have brought him home last night as I know I didn't."

"He must be the guy I was drinking with last night. I guess I had better get rid of him."

As we now had two hours before classes were to start, I wasn't sure just how Harvey was going to accomplish mission impossible. At eight I was ready for school and left, leaving Harvey with his dilemma. During the first period Mr. Henheffer came to my room to see if I knew of Harvey's whereabouts. I assured him that when I left; Harvey was getting ready to come to school. A phone call to the apartment went unanswered and a substitute teacher was quickly arranged. We didn't see Harvey for another four days. His solution to that morning's situation was to suggest to our guest that they go for a beer, which became a ninety-six hour solution

Despite a few other escapades, Harvey survived to the end of the year but our sharing relationship didn't. In April I gave up the apartment and moved to Calgary where I rented a house where Lawrie and I would live after we were married. Harvey moved to Okotoks, the next town up the line, where he could frequent the bar to his hearts content.

In the summer of nineteen sixty-five Lawrie and I were married and C.I.D.A. came through with an assignment to

Uganda for the following year. We moved into our house in Calgary and Lawrie continued her career as Women's Editor for the Calgary Herald and I commuted to High River. The commute proved interesting in that I would leave the city early in the morning having first dropped Lawrie at her work place. I would proceed down the Macloud Trail at the same time as the milk delivery vans were setting out on their deliveries. I am convinced that as time went on the drivers recognized my car and we would jockey for position and race to the city limits where they dispersed. Lawrie, to this day, says it was just a figment of my imagination. We would line up at the intersection waiting for the light to turn green. Our wheels spun and we roared down the road like a group of formula one race cars seeking the win which would give you the points that would conclude in the world championship of milk van racing. Regardless whether the van drivers were truly in on it or not it always made my day, especially after a win, as I felt I had already accomplished something that day.

That following year the new social studies teacher, Ross Dumville, came on staff. He was unmarried and lived in Calgary with his parents. We agreed that we could cut expenses by alternating vehicles on a weekly basis. This worked well except in early spring when Ross, who drove an Austin Healey, insisted on driving to work with the top down. Plus six Celsius at one hundred kilometers per hour turns into a bloody cold ride even if you're wrapped up like an Eskimo in a blizzard. I guess I was just soft as Ross would climb out and, with a big smile on his rosy red face that was the same color as his fiery red hair, would stride vigorously into the school.

We had a reasonably uneventful commute that year except for two incidents worthy of note. The first occurred returning to Calgary one evening when my car decided to throw a radiator fan bearing, allowing the fan to slice through the radiator. We were lucky in that we were rescued by a couple of Mormon missionaries returning home after a little rural door knocking.

The next day Ross took his car but only a few blocks from home it went into total discharge. We returned to his house where his father suggested we take his car. So off we went again feeling a little pressed for time. This time we almost made the edge of town when it too, died a sudden death. We abandoned it and made our way to the south side Greyhound bus station, which luckily wasn't that far away. Ross phoned his father to inform him of the good news and I phoned the school to say we were going to be late. We caught the bus, scheduled to get us to High River around ten. Feeling a little tense after all the excitement of three breakdowns within twenty-four hours, we settled back and left the driving to them. The driving however, came to an abrupt stop ten miles from our destination. We were all ordered off and the driver disappeared behind the bus with a fire extinguisher. The motor compartment was engulfed in flames but was quickly brought under control. We were allowed back on the inoperable bus and the driver hitched a ride to the nearest service station to summon up another. We finally arrived around noon. As Shakespeare, in his writings said, " All's well that ends well".

The second incident I wasn't involved in luckily. Ross was staying after school so I decided to take my own vehicle. Ross, having finished his after-school activity, went and had a beer with another teacher. After, driving out of town, he rounded a corner and that was the last thing he remembered until he regained consciousness. Looking up he found himself peering into a large number of huge watery eyes. For a moment he thought he was having a close encounter of the third kind, but soon realized he was looking into the eyes of a herd of cows that had gathered round to view this flying object that had landed in their pasture. He was fortunate. Maybe if we had both been in the car, fate may not have been so kind.

When you are fortunate to work in communities where the parents are happy with the school's performance, you and the students have a much better attitude towards school and the learning process. This was certainly true of High River and much credit must go to an informed school board and a solid administration. When I arrived in High River the laboratory was well set up, much to the credit of my predecessor. However its one shortcoming was the microscopes. There were not enough and the ones we had were of poor quality. When I placed a request for eight new ones at around four to five hundred dollars each, it pushed the science budget beyond its limit. The principal sat down with me and suggested we purchase a lesser number. I explained that four students assigned to each microscope was too many and would inhibit carrying out the expectations of the curriculum. Being an understanding man he resubmitted the request and the matter was referred to the board. I was asked to attend the next board meeting and to bring along one the microscopes presently in use. I took along slides and some specimens we were expected to view and reproduce on paper in class. I was feeling a little anxious about the exercise, as I had never been placed before a board to argue my case for equipment. When my turn came, I set up the equipment and invited the members to view the situation for themselves. One member was a medical doctor and, upon examining and viewing the material, suggested the request be honored immediately. When people in these positions attack a problem from a results point of view rather than budget, the quality of education in the area can be reflected in quality of performance. The students found the microscopes intriguing and very revealing. They appreciated the fact that holders of the purse strings were truly concerned that the student's welfare and education came ahead of the almighty dollar.

The students worked hard and most times without complaint. When the students feel that others are concerned and interested in what they do, they in turn live up to the expectations of the community. What the students possibly don't realize is that this is all done to assure they do well. Another aspect that comes to the fore is the attitude of the student towards the teacher. The teacher is the authority figure and therefore is often kept at arms length. In this school the teacher was held in respect and yet there was good camaraderie. As a teacher you develop a genuine fondness for these young people in your care and you feel a great loss when one is lost to death. Although no student actually died while I was in High River, one did shortly after I left. Her name was Connie Palmer, an excellent yet quiet student. She was one of the few students who had solid thoughts about her future. It was with great sadness that I learned she had died from cancer. It is things like this that make you wonder if there is any rhyme or reason to life. After two very pleasant years I left High River, not because I wanted to but because I was given an assignment to teach in Uganda, Africa, an assignment I couldn't refuse

Vic and Lawrie's Wedding

July 17. 1965, United Church, Drumheller, Alberta

Chapter 7

OFF TO UGANDA

Dr. Livingston I presume? No it's me.

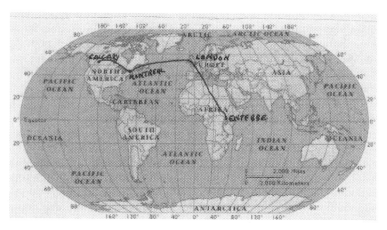

Our route to Uganda took us from Calgary, Alberta to Montreal, Quebec. From Montreal to London, England then from London to Entebbe, Uganda.

L AWRIE AND I married on July 17, 1965 and we lived in Calgary after my episode with Harvey. Harvey moved on to other things I guess but I have no idea what or where. As previously related, things went well in sixty-five and sixty-six, the exception being the death of my father. He died of cancer at age sixty-seven. Although a great loss in my life, it is life and you have to move on. I had applied to C.I.D.A. before our marriage and Lawrie was delighted at the prospect of going overseas again, she having returned from an around the world trip and a stay in New Zealand for a year and a half. Now a year and a half later we were looking at some traveling again. In the spring of sixty-six the word came that I had received a posting to Busoga College, Mwiri, Jinja Uganda. The atlas came out to locate this place called Jinja. We were delighted to find that it was located at the source of the Nile on Lake Victoria, the location that Speke discovered, our history books state. Speke may have discovered it as far as the Europeans were concerned but the indigenous people had known it was there centuries before. The one thing traveling abroad does for you is make you realize that the persons inhabiting the area before the all knowing white man came had a very extensive history of their own. The fact that we taught them that we had discovered it seemed a bit presumptuous on our part and a little ridiculous on theirs.

That summer I left High River School with a degree of sadness. Lawrie, now quite pregnant, resigned from the Calgary Herald and we spent time visiting relatives and preparing to leave. All our vaccinations, etc., out of the way, Lawrie stayed with her parents and I headed for Montreal for a two week orientation conference. Here we received the dos and don'ts of living in a foreign country and the horrendous effects of culture shock. Certainly some things seemed a little out of the ordinary; such as if you are unfortunate enough to run down and kill or badly injure a person, don't stop. If you do the locals would take out their revenge on you by taking your life. This did seem like a good reason to keep on trekking. This was not a racial thing because they would exact the same punishment on their own kind. This was substantiated by a situation that happened while we were there. Despite such situations we were told the people were very friendly and outgoing, a characteristic we found to be true.

The orientation went well and on the whole was very informative and gave us a chance to meet other teachers going to the East African area. It also became an eye opener into our own cultural composition. As a westerner, I found it amazing how the residents in such a cosmopolitan area used French and English like one language. Sitting in a bar one evening with a group from the course, it was frustrating to eavesdrop on the persons at the next table telling a joke which they started in English and ended in French or vise versa. Now if we all had that ability I am sure this French-English thing would disappear at a much faster rate

Our wives joined us for the last few days before we shipped out and they too were versed in the things to expect. However, the cultural shock never turned out to be as great as we were led to believe and the whole adventure was something Lawrie and I would consider being one of the highlights of our lives. We boarded our aircraft heading for Britain, which was also an exciting event as it meant I would be returning to the land of my birth for the first time in seventeen years. I guess regardless of how adamantly Canadian I had become, there was still a little feeling of national pride for the country in which I had spent the first eleven years of my life. The trip to Britain was great, as complimentary drinks had been laid on for us and all enjoyed a great deal of cordiality and fun, some more than others. One fellow, whose family consisted of two young daughters, had an exceptionally good time, until the plane landed next morning and he, blurry eyed and hung over, got off hanging onto the hands of his bouncy, vibrant daughters full of questions and things they wanted to see and do, including seeing the Queen.

We didn't have the same problem as our only child was still in the womb.

Feeling a fair degree of excitement at being in England, although not quite at the point where I felt like kneeling down and kissing the ground, we encountered our first British natives. Talk about culture shock. Not only did it seem foreign but I had a great deal of difficulty understanding what was once my mother tongue. However, through sign language and snippets that did resemble the Canadian language in some small way, we found our bus and were whisked off to our hotel. As beautiful as it had looked from the air and knowing all the wonderful cultural attributes, spending twelve hours there made me realize why immigration to Canada was such a great move on the part of my parents.

The following day we were in transit to Uganda and eight hours later we landed at Entebbe Airport. The first thing that hit us when the aircraft door opened was an odor in the air that was a combination of the equatorial heat and the unique smells of Africa. Just as our own homes and environments have their own distinctive smells, it is also true of other countries and continents. Along with the smell came two persons dressed in some form of uniform carrying what appeared to be large aerosol cans, the contents of which they sprayed liberally up and down the cabin. Once this operation was completed we were allowed to disembark. Our passports carried the notation that we were members of the Canadian aid program and we were to be extended all the cooperation possible. This seemed to work as we were whisked through customs and into a waiting car to be taken to Kampala and a stay over night before being taken to Busoga College.

Uganda and Busoga College Mwiri

We arrived at the Grand Hotel and were greeted by an exuberant, friendly and efficient staff all beaming that big toothy smile so prevalent among Uganda's population. Our accommodation was first class, I suppose due to the colonial British who had the hotels built and were the only ones rich enough to stay in them. Regardless, we kicked back, thankful for the peace and quite after our thirty hours of travel. The lunch hour arrived and we toddled down to a beautiful dining patio, where masses of blooms covered the flowering trees and shrubs which supplied a cool and refreshing atmosphere. No sooner had we been seated than our waiter was upon us ready to serve our every need. At this point the need seemed to be a long cool drink. Anything you required was available but our waiter suggested that we try the local drink, Waragi, a gin or vodka like liquor made from bananas.. This combined with limejuice proved to be just what the doctor ordered, well not in Lawrie's case being as she was six months pregnant. In those days we were not very wise to the problems of combining the two. Luckily nothing drastic happened from her having a few drinks as our son Doug turned out as normal as could have been expected from the combining of our genes. Lunch was not hamburger and chips but a three-course meal starting with fish, then meat and finally fresh fruit. This was the general fare for evening dinner as well, only dinner was much more elaborate. God! We both thought, if this is culture shock we are all for it.

The next day we were collected by a car from the Ministry of Education to be driven to Busoga College Mwiri, about sixty miles to the east. We were not sure whether traveling by road in Uganda is consider part of culture shock or not, but it was at the time hellishly scary. Driving seemed to involve making up your own rules of the road as you went along. If it was not safe to pass on the correct side, pass on the other or if a lorry (truck) was going too fast to pass on the level, wait until his load slowed him down going up hill, then pass. Pedestrians seldom sauntered across the road and if they did, a good blast on the horn sent them scurrying for safety. I always maintained there were no deaf persons in Uganda for obvious reasons. As some indication of the driving style, statistics at the time stated that there were two deaths per million-road mile driven in Canada and ninety-two per million road miles in Uganda. It was not uncommon to be passed by a taxi designed to carry eight to nine people carrying twelve to fourteen passengers, at speeds in excess of sixty miles per hour, only for it to stop suddenly in front of you without warning. So went our ride along this winding narrow road. Our driver was somewhat puzzled by Lawrie's muffled screams, deep gasps and involuntary braking motions with her foot. I must admit that although I was more outwardly calm, my insides were going through the same motions. As exciting as we found the ride, we also found having to stop at police road checks a little upsetting, although not as upsetting as when the army with their loaded sub machine guns took over in times of crisis. Despite the car ride that could only be compared to the devil's spiral at the carnival, the trip was something that remains in our minds eye to this day.

The earth was a bright red-brown color much like the soil found in PEI, and was locally known as murrum. This created the backdrop against which small mud huts sprouted up between groves of bananas, papaya, and mangoes. The yards were all beautifully swept, and little stools and wooden chairs were randomly set about. Chickens and goats ran freely about, intermingling with numerous children. One could catch a glimpse of a mother returning from a well or stream, often some distance away, with a huge pot balanced on a ring of woven banana leaves on top of her head. The men sat in some of the chairs, seeming to contribute little or nothing to the activity going on around them. The men's sole contribution to the family seemed to be nothing more than contributing sperm to produce more progeny. Then the scene would change to non-occupied land interspersed with trees and bushes, often covered with vast arrays of beautiful blossoms. Then a small village appeared with several small stores called dukas, which sold all kinds of articles needed by the surrounding inhabitants. From this it changed to a well-cultivated sugar plantation, then next you were plunged into a tropical rain forest, with small streams, the banks crowded by a host of magnificent butterflies, either settled or milling around in clouds of psychedelic color. In the high branches monkeys frolicked with gay abandon, screaming obscenities at the passing traffic. Our car moved out of the forest and a few miles further was stopped at the first police check on top of the Owen Falls dam, the source of all the electric power for the country. Located just below Ripon Falls, which no longer existed, it is the point where the White Nile tumbles out of Lake Victoria. After a quick check we moved on past Jinja via a bypass and east again towards our destination. Four large hills dominated the area and atop each a group of buildings. These were schools built by the missionaries to convert and educate the locals. Our driver pointed to the most easterly and told us it was Busoga College. The schools were build on hills for two reasons, the first to keep the students, as in those days most were boys, away from the villages and the booze and women and secondly, to avoid the malaria carrying mosquitoes which didn't relish the high altitudes.

Lawrie and I looked at one another and at the hill cradling our new home on its summit and I think we both knew we were starting an adventure, which was to become one, if not the most, exciting part of our lives together. This was Africa and we already had found an attachment to the Dark Continent

An aerial view of Busoga College Mwiri

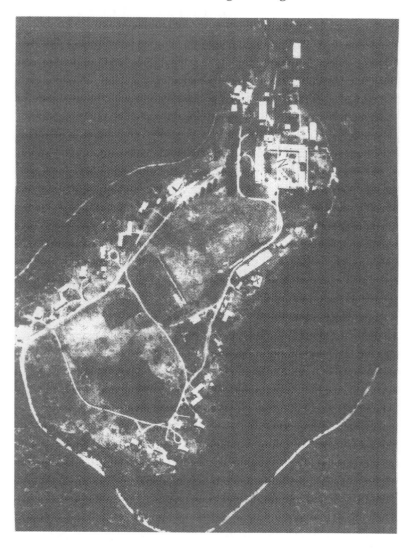

Our house is marked with an X
Brewer House with a Y
Instruction area marked with a Z

Chapter 8

BUSOGA COLLEGE MWIRI

Seven hundred feet above Lake Victoria,
a place of higher learning.

THE CAR slowed and swung on to a murrum road. It soon started its assent up the hill leaving clouds of red dust, burying any person trudging up the hill in its red smoke screen. We reached the top. The road leveled out revealing a flat tabletop plateau. A view of the campus showed two large playing field areas surrounded by a ring road. On the outer edge of the road staff house were alternated with the dormitories. All the dormitories were empty, as the students were on summer break and wouldn't be returning for another week or so. At the far end of the hill were the school buildings, some of which were the original structures. To one side stood an old thatched roofed building and a sign reading OFFICE.

Dan Okunga, his wife Ida and their children

Seconds after we stopped a small round-faced man appeared, a broad Ugandan smile on his face. This was the headmaster, Daniel Okunga, one of the first African headmasters of such a prestigious school in the country. He greeted us warmly and asked if we had had a pleasant trip. He hoped our stay at the school would be long and pleasant. He told us we would be billeted with a family who had agreed to keep us and initiate us to the ways of the school, until such time as the rest of our belongings arrived. The Struthers had agreed to take on this onerous task. The family consisted of David, Moira and their three children Graham, Andrew and Hazel. They were a Scottish family and unlike the well-known stereotype, were generous and accepting, despite the fact that I was a displaced Englishman.

During the days that followed, we met other staff members and had a chance to look over the school facilities. The classrooms were very plain, consisting of a desk or demonstration table and wooden benches and tables. Imagine the hue and cry were our Canadian students subjected to such bleak conditions, and yet learning went on here far surpassing that occurring in many of our North American facilities. David filled me in on some things of which I should be aware. The fact that the first year students didn't learn a great deal in the first month for the following reasons: firstly their grasp of the English language along with our strange accents made it virtually impossible for them to understand us and, secondly, they were too shy to ask questions if they didn't understand. This soon changed and in contrast, he told me, the boys returning to the school knew the syllabus of each course by heart and if they felt you were not doing a good job of teaching, they were not beyond going on strike and would refuse to return to class until the situation was remedied. This news, of course, relaxed me to the point where I had nightmares of facing an empty classroom with angry students burning me in effigy outside. This, I am glad to say, never happened to me or any other teacher at our school while I was there. However, it did occur at some other schools. We came close to a general strike over some rule changes during the unsettled times of the Amin coup, which I shall relate later.

Another aspect that gave me some concern was the fact it had been a missionary school and some of the teachers were of the missionary ilk. As Lawrie and I were both agnostic, we felt we may well be on the outside and considered not quite proper. Most staff members were of the Christian faith but did not consider their teaching assignment to include religious conversion. Since the school's inception, the Church Missionary Society or CMS, a branch of the Church of England, had been its main supporters and operators. The previous headmaster, the Rev. Jack Coates, was the last headmaster to be appointed by the CMS and a school ran according to CMS policy. Although many Ugandans may not have received an education had it not been for such schools, it was designed to instill the white man's beliefs and life style. Everyone was obligated to go to church on Sunday, no booze was openly displayed in any of the staff houses but nonetheless was consumed. Tea parties were very formal, where the ladies wore white gloves and hats. It was known that the Rev. Coates did, on occasion, wear his pith helmet in true British colonial style. The morals of everyone were expected to be of the traditional British standard, and this carried over to the African help that did the domestic and menial task on the school compound.

One story that illustrates this, involved an American teacher, Paul Anderson, who had just left Busoga College before we arrived. The headmaster's wife approached Paul one day, saying," I see your houseboy has a young lady living with him.

"I guess so", Paul replied in a casual American manner.

"Do you know if they are married"? Ask Mrs. Coates.

"I am not sure," replied Paul, not quite sure what was coming next.

"Have you seen their marriage certificate?" She asked.

"No", said Paul, "but then come to think of it I haven't seen yours either".

This brought an abrupt end to the conversation and she returned to her realm of a more traditional sanctuary, where people took such matters seriously.

Luckily Daniel Okunga, although a Christian, was more concerned with academic achievement than the missionary zeal of the former administration. This alleviated a lot of pressure and the possible conflict that may well have shortened my stay, had the Rev. Coates still been involved. Daniel was not only a man that had a good understanding of people and thus his staff, but he was also blessed with a great sense of humor, or should I say a good understanding of western humor, as the humor of different cultures varies to a large degree. On one occasion we were having what was called an "adjectives" meeting (a meeting to discuss the boys' progress). A situation occurred that made the need for understanding fact on one hand and intent on the other became abundantly clear. Speaking of one student who apparently excelled in English, Ozzie Butler, one of the English teachers on staff described the student as "working like a nigger". The room went deadly silent; and Ozzie, realizing his gaff, was seeking to pour some oil on the water.

Daniel smiled and said, "I am pleased to hear that he is working so hard and that the young lad is showing such zeal and enthusiasm."

Dan knew the slip of the tongue was only an expression of exuberance and pleasure on Ozzie's part at having such a great student in class and not a racial slur. He smoothed it over by expressing pleasure the student was applying himself so well to his studies.

One concern to me was the fact that, during the eleven years I lived in England, I never passed my "eleven plus" examinations. It restricted me from attending grammar school and university in England. All the teachers at Mwiri were British or were Africans who had trained in Britain. All were extremely well qualified and had proven themselves very acceptable to the student body. Here was I, a newcomer, a Canadian (the first ever on staff) and above all I had not done as well academically in school as was obvious of all the other teachers at Busoga College. My concern was, could I hold up my end in such a great academic group? Certainly many of the staff members were educated well beyond my basic B.Ed degree. My ability to work with people, both students and teachers alike, had stood me in good stead in Canada; a situation I hoped would help me here. Fortunately it did and enabled me to do a job of which I could be proud. The students, as the following years proved, were satisfied this Canadian teacher could do the job. Another Canadian teacher named Dean McKenzie, an extremely clever and intellectual person, came to our school a year or two later and enhanced the image of Canadian teachers even further.

Chapter 9

THE STUDENTS RETURN

What am I doing here?

THE DAY came when the students returned; a well-dressed group indeed. The lower form boys were dressed in sparkling white shirts and shorts, whereas the higher school members had gray slacks, even whiter white shirts and blue blazers. They seemed to range in age from fourteen to thirty, some of the older students having had their education interrupted by a lack of funds. Each student was expected to pay around six hundred shillings or one hundred dollars per term, which was an astronomical amount and required the whole village to pool resources to send a student to such a prestigious institution. In some cases the funds could not be raised and the student would need to sit out a term or two, until such times as money became available. This may seem like a hefty contribution for the villagers to make, as it was. However, they expected their graduates to make repayment several times over and also to assist others with subsequent school fees as needed. So it was really an investment for the village in the future of their youth and their community. The overall effect was that the students worked extremely hard for the privilege of being able to attend. This may give a lot of credence to following such a system here in North America but of course it would only lead to education only for the rich, for we certainly know the North American village would never make the effort to raise the funds as they did there. I still dream about how great it would be if we had that drive and enthusiasm in all of our students in Canada, a place where we have the resources and no one is prevented from attending school because of a lack of funds.

Almost six hundred students arrived, which resulted in a great deal of excitement and chatter. I did not perceive at first that tribalism and color did create barriers among the boys. The boys referred to each other as that black boy or that brown boy, which to me in my first encounter wasn't that obvious. What I did notice was they did appear very much alike and hard to distinguish from one another. One reason was that they shared many similar characteristics, like the tight curly black hair, brown eyes, broad noses, and in most cases, very slim, athletic bodies. I wondered if we, the white race, all looked alike to them, although it's hard to believe we do, as we are such a mongrel race by comparison. The discipline and manners were also evident immediately. Every teacher was automatically treated with respect. This did two things: one, you didn't have to spend time trying to convince them you deserved it, and two, it created a healthy relationship between student and teacher and this immediately set the tone for what each expected of the other. During the five years I spent in Uganda, I never saw one case where the teacher lost the respect of the students, mainly because the teacher worked hard to protect that respect. On the other hand, the teachers had a great deal of respect for the students. An outstanding result of this was I never had to discipline a student for the entire five years I taught at Busoga College. If we contrast this with North American schools, where the teacher has to earn the respect, then there is always a challenge and often a conflict between teacher and student. The other side of the coin is that here many students do not earn the respect of the teacher; the offshoot of this is more discipline problems. Add to this, when discipline problems arise, the intervention of parents, which often further erodes the respect and cooperation of all parties involved. The result is less education and more conflict. Our problem in the western world is everyone is an "expert" because each went through the system and therefore knows how it works, or thinks so. None of this existed in the Ugandan schools and as a result my observation was that the students were top-level students. My education from this was that mutual respect is so important in the learning situation. When I became a principal in Canada, my opening day remarks always included the statement that every teacher in the school must have the student's respect and likewise the teacher for the student. This didn't solve all the problems but I always felt it helped establish a more congenial relationship. Such a statement of conduct was totally unnecessary in the Ugandan school.

The actions were in some cases a little extreme for my taste, as students immediately stood up when you came into the room, the scrapping of chairs on the concrete floor was more than I wanted to hear. A curt good morning class, with good morning sir was adequate. One negative aspect that occurred was that the students were sometimes too subservient. There were times when they would seek out teachers to borrow money, especially if they thought you were a bit, of a soft touch. Lawrie and I may have fit into that category, but what we found annoying was the groveling stance and manner they took when asking. I must admit I felt like giving them a swift kick, but we also came to realize that this was part of their culture, enhanced by the Europeans and Asians in the country. Interestingly I found the longer we stayed, the less we really understood their way of thinking, and I feel that was also true in reverse. It takes a great deal of hard work to try and understand why they thought the way they did, and therefore, it is much easier to dismiss their actions as being that of the third world under-privileged group, a child like mind or numerous other comments or phrases we use to get around the fact we don't want to make the effort to try and understand.

As I didn't want to be considered an easy mark I adopted the plan of hiring the student to earn the money he needed. It seemed to work and in most cases we were both happy with the arrangement. I came to know several of the boys quite well in this way, and in fact some of the work time became a time of very interesting conversation. They seemed to enjoy talking about their families, their ambitions and the particular area of Uganda from which they came. They, in turn, would quiz me about Canada.

Our last staff meeting before classes began outlined the timetable we would follow and the classroom where the subject was to be taught. Besides this, we were also given the name of the dormitory for which we were responsible. I was assigned as housemaster to Brewer House, named after one of the former headmasters in days past. Despite my feelings about missionaries, I couldn't help admiring the guts and fortitude they had to carry out the tasks set for them in an area so isolated and unfamiliar. These people were strong, almost fearless, and helped in the colonization of these areas covered by the Union Jack.

Brewer House, of which I was housemaster

The then headmaster of the farm school, which was located at the bottom of our hill, and his wife, Mr. and Mrs. Woods, exemplified this fearlessness. A thief in Uganda was not uncommon, yet the locals treated it with extremely harsh measures. If a person was suspected of robbery, a hue and cry would go up and everybody would chase after the suspect. If caught the person or persons would be killed. The Woods were driving into Jinja one day when down the road came a large group chasing three suspected thieves. The Woods stopped and tried to get the three in their car. At this point rocks were flying through the air and Mrs. Woods pulled one to the ground and covered him with her body. Mr. Woods, having got two in the car, returned to help his wife rescue the third, but not before a rock hit her hand, and broke her finger. The three managed to return to the car and then drive through the milling crowd, amidst waving fist and flying rocks. Once clear they drove the three individuals to the police station, where they were turned over to the authorities. The immense courage this took is beyond my imagination.

The task of the housemaster was not too arduous as it involved assuring the boys basic needs were met. Also you were expected to be a confidant and advisor and, a role I failed to fulfill, spiritual leader. This task involved leading the boys in prayer each evening, I solved the problem by letting those who wished to have an evening assembly to do so and the others and myself could do their own thing. It was obviously a cop out on my part, but better that than being a bigger hypocrite than I already was. The boys also seemed to like the arrangement, particularly those who didn't follow the Christian faith. Once a week I dropped in and we would have a type of roundtable on things that may have become a concern. There was a house leader who also conversed with me when a need arose, so I felt everything was in hand, especially as our own dwelling and Brewer House were only a hundred yards apart.

The staff meeting also delegated other chores. Each master, as we were known, was given areas of responsibility. When we moved into our own house, the only one with a fireplace (which we used a few times), we found we didn't have hot water. The hot water heater had been nonfunctional for many years apparently. If one wanted a bath it was necessary for the houseboy to boil the water. As at that point we didn't have a houseboy and were unsure whether we would get one, we weren't excited about the idea of having to boil water every time we wished a bath. I decided to investigate the problem and found the old heating coil spring element had burned off from the terminal. In town I found a small clamp like device that one uses on the end of a curtain rod. I fixed it by placing the terminal and the end of the element inside the clamp and tightening the screw. Checking it, the circuit seemed complete, so the heater was reassembled and turned on. It worked and continued to do so for the rest of the time we were there and, I suspect, for a number of years into the future. The upshot of this was I became the electricity master, which led to some interesting situations, things one would end up in jail for in Canada.

Lawrie and I still were not sure we wanted to become so colonial as to have a houseboy: we liked the term "steward" instead of house boy. However, we had a constant stream of applicants, which made us realize this was a major source of employment, and now we felt obligated to help decrease the unemployment rate as well as make our lives a great deal more pleasant. Not knowing how to select a competent person, we asked each one to return on a certain date and from that group we would make our selection. When that day came only one showed up. He was the only one with a good understanding of English with a Canadian accent and the knowledge to follow the instructions. We hired him immediately. We certainly lucked out, for Yokobo, a Sudanese native, was very competent and good at his job as well as having a solid understanding of the mzungu's (white man's) humor. We thought we had died and gone to heaven. In the morning we could have awakened to tea in bed, but declined. However, we did arise to find the living and dining room spotlessly cleaned and breakfasts already to be served. One felt like asking for a peeled grape, but never did.

The scene was set for the beginning of the school term. The house had hot water, our houseboy, as we also came to call him, was in place, and Lawrie, now very large with our first child, settled in to wait. I, on the other hand was off to meet my first class, not as cock sure and full of pride as I had been on my first day in Claresholm.

Students and Buildings at Busoga College

Chapter 10

THE FIRST DAY OF A PERFECT FIVE YEARS

What? I don't have an accent!

B USOGA COLLEGE was one of the few schools to teach both O level and A level courses. The O level was a four-year program equivalent to the grade eight to eleven level in Canada, whereas A level was grade twelve and first year university. I was assigned to teach some of the O Level biology, chemistry and one course in first year geography. The biology and chemistry courses were straightforward and I didn't expect to have any major problems. The first year geography would be a little more challenging. I was sure that most if not all of the boys knew a great deal more about the geography of the area than I. I knew as well that it was very unlikely I was going to be challenged by any of the first year students in the class, at least for the first month or so. Doing some quick research I learned as much basic Ugandan geography as I could. This seemed to hold me in good stead but what I didn't realize was that our particular area was a little microcosm of its own. The lesson one day was on the climatic cycles that occurred in East Africa. At this point a huge black cloud gathered overhead, lightning flashed, thunder roared and the water coming off the roof could only be compared to standing under Niagara Falls. And I was trying to tell them with some authority that this was the dry season.

My very first class on the first day on the job was with a third form class in biology. As I entered the room the boys all sprang to their feet, stools scraping noisily across the concrete floor, and in chorus sang out, "Good morning sir". I responded with a cheery good morning of my own, asked them to be seated. Everyone now seated I requested that in future I would prefer only the greeting without the noisy standing process. I don't know if they thought that this weird guy was going to have them do a number of things differently from the accepted tradition or not. I didn't with this one exception.

I introduced myself verbally, not on the blackboard as on my very first day in the classroom. I told them that I was Canadian and that I was not accustomed to their ways of operation, but that I would do my best to learn quickly and I was open to any help or advice they wished to send my way. None came. This opening procedure happened in every class throughout the day and I reiterated my remarks. They accepted me for what I was and I couldn't have asked for anything better. How different it seemed as I stared out over the class to focus on a mass of black faces, giving no indication of how they were reacting to the pale face in front of them.

"Well gentlemen we may as well get started". Small grins appeared. I was not quite sure why. Was it my strange accent, or the fact I had called them gentlemen. This may have been it for, a year or two later, a friend of mine was stopped by an African policeman for going through a stop sign. Ax Benzon is quite a character and when the policeman came up to his car, Ax asked him why he had stopped him.

"You went through the stop sign", the policeman said.

"I am sure I stopped", said Ax.

"Do you think you stopped"? The policeman was now a little unsure he was right.

"I am definitely sure I stopped," repeated Ax".

"I see", said the policeman, "you are a gentleman, you may go".

Ax thanked the constable but before leaving turned to him and asked. "What is a gentleman?'

The policeman replied, "It is a man who wears fine clothes and drives a motorcar".

So looking back, this may have also been their definition of a gentleman; whatever, my statement evoked a grin and to get a reaction at all I thought was a good start.

We started the lesson by outlining what had to be covered that term, something they already knew, but at least we were working from a base of understanding. To further expand this base I asked a series of questions about what they had studied the previous term, and then quizzed them on some aspects of the work. They had a good grasp of the past work and the questions I asked established the fact that my understanding of the subject material was also adequate. The lesson I had planned seemed to go over well, the students were so anxious to learn. The beating of the drum ended the class the same way it had begun. No shrill bell just the rhythmic tum-tum-ta-ta-tum.

The classes came and went, until that afternoon, when I encountered my first, first year class. The usual good afternoon sir, as stools scrapped across the floor. I launched into my "do not stand" speech. I repeated the instructions several times, keeping in mind what Dave Struthers had told me about the lack of understanding English with an accent. When they had a full understanding of my instructions we pushed on with the class. I would give some instruction complemented with written notes and illustrations. Periodically I would ask, "Are there any questions?" They sat there stoically with bright eyes, and shiny white teeth appearing through slightly smiling faces. I would then repeat the material just in case there were some who hadn't grasped the main points. So the lesson went, me unsure whether I was actually getting through or not. At one point, stopping to enquire if anyone needed more explanation, I spotted a brown arm shoot to the sky.

"Yes", I asked?

"Please sir, would you mind going over that last point again, I'm afraid I didn't grasp the relevance between this and the last point you were making ".

Not only was it phrased in better English than I was often able to muster, but with the most deliberate Oxford English accent. I hadn't noticed a little white English boy in the room and there wasn't. It was Zigazooka the son of a Ugandan diplomat, who had spent several years in England. Later I discovered Zigazooka had spent six or more years in the English school system. He was sharp as a tack and quick to question things he didn't understand. Although teaching him was hardly a challenge, I realized that if he didn't understand, I could be very sure that none or very few of the others did. This gave me some guide as to my success as well as providing a sounding board off which I could bounce questions as a means of repeating segments of the lesson without making it obvious that I was assuming the rest had not comprehended the material. This procedure did not have to go on very long, for in a very short period the confidence of the rest of the class had increased dramatically and their eagerness to learn soon overcame any fear (but not a lowering of respect) they had of this authority figure imparting information to them.

It was exciting because the information was information they had not heard before or if they had, it was on a very limited basis. I am sure that is why grade one teachers enjoy their assignment so much. Here, like a flower unfolding you can see them absorbing the knowledge you are imparting, knowledge no one else has had a part in placing in their minds. After grade one you are never sure whether it was you or someone prior to you who gave them the information and understanding. Likewise, I knew any biological science information they learned was more than likely the result of my doing. This is when examination results give you a good understanding of how well you are doing.

I have never in my entire teaching career experienced such enthusiasm and willingness to work as these students showed both in class and in the labs. Assignments given were always in on time and done with as much thoroughness as each student could muster. You set out your expectations and they worked with every ounce of energy to meet those expectations. If they made mistakes and the mistakes were pointed out, you could almost be assured that the mistake would not be repeated. My God, I thought I had died and gone to heaven. Without a word of a lie the teaching experience in Uganda spoiled me for the rest of my teaching career.

Under the C.I.D.A. contract we were not allowed to stay more than five years, for fear we would be tempted to become permanent expatriates, and I can assure you it could well have happened.

Chapter 11

DOUG THE PUG

All that hard work finally paying off.

WHEN WE arrived in Uganda Lawrie was seven months pregnant and was close to not being able to travel. Many thought she should have stayed in Canada to have the baby, rather than in this primitive African country. However, Lawrie being an adventurous type decided it would be okay. We were lucky as Jinja had several good doctors and among them was a superb obstetrician. Time passed and on November nineteenth, nineteen sixty-six, a Saturday, we went to Jinja as usual for our weekly shopping expedition. Having picked up our groceries, among which was a case of twenty five-quart bottles of beer (their "six-pack") we made our way back home. Yokobo had lunch ready for us and I had just settled in to eat my soup, when Lawrie announced we had to go to the hospital.

"Hang on a minute", I said, "I just want to finish my soup".

"Now", she said with determination in her voice, "or I will be having it here".

As that didn't totally appeal to me, we set out for Jinja once more. As we headed down the hill Lawrie shouted, "go faster." This sounded serious as she was always yelling at me to slow down. We hit the main road and still she was prompting me to step on it. We arrived at the hospital without mishap and in record time. Once there she was rushed inside. The nurse on the desk asked me to fill out the admittance forms, which I did quickly, because I was planning on witnessing the birth. I handed them in at the desk and was about to head for the delivery room when a nurse met me and announced I had a son, seven pounds and twelve ounces and twenty-two and a half inches long. He was a long skinny baby and had slipped out like a snake with no great how do you do. He hasn't changed a lot except he is now six foot five and weights a hundred and sixty pounds.

Lawrie and the baby were shortly placed in a hospital room, furnished much like a motel, with its own bathroom and on top of this she was given a menu from which to chose her various meals. I tell you things were sure primitive, unlike the luxurious conditions she would have enjoyed in Canada.

This was not the general rule for the Ugandan at large. Most were relegated to the third class level, which was a large room containing numerous beds, a common bathroom and your food was prepared by a relative, who camped outside the hospital gates. Are we sure that we want a two or three tier system here in Canada? Babies were considered to be a rather normal happening and long stays in the hospital were unheard of, unless there were complications. So on the morning of the third day Lawrie came home with our new baby boy.

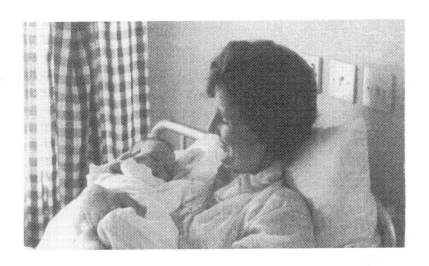

Baby Douglas enjoying his first day of life on Earth

Douglas and his protector Marty Monk

Marty our monkey became immediately attached to the baby and was Doug's prime protector, not allowing anyone near the baby buggy. He would sit on the edge of the buggy, tail high in the air, back arched, big black eyes glaring out from under a protruding eyebrow ridge and his mouth open, showing gleaming white and sharp canine teeth. No one looked in the buggy until we assured Marty it was okay to allow a peek at the baby. When Lawrie's mom and dad came to Uganda shortly after Doug was born, Jimmy, Lawrie's father, would declare that you had to have a tail to get any attention around our house. From this point of view the gecko lizards that were part of every household didn't get much attention as Marty, in an attempt to catch them would grab them by the tail. The tail would immediately break off and he would be left with this wiggling appendage in his hand. Marty, however, thought that half a gecko was better than no gecko at all and ate this delicacy with glee.

Monkeys and babies weren't the only new thing around our home, as we had also acquired a chameleon. His home was between the window and the screen. In the bottom we had placed a few rocks, which supported a branch that reached to the top of the window. Here Cam as he was called, could climb about to look out on the world and enjoy fresh air from the outside. He was well supplied with grasshoppers by Lawrie and I and Yokobo, whom I felt was not only an excellent houseboy but also a born naturalist. This seemed to work well for Cam, until one day we noticed the window was slightly ajar and Cam was nowhere to be found. We should have kept it quiet; because when Lawrie's mother found out she spent the next couple of days walking around the house like someone expecting to be attacked by some man-eating monster. I don't believe she slept, a situation that wasn't helped by the fact a gecko fell off the ceiling into the bed with Chrissy in it, something they usually never do. The situation brought on the same reaction as if a mouse had run across her bed and it took two stiff brandies to settle her nerves. She remained on constant alert, as Cam was still at large, although we tried to alleviate her fears by assuring her he must have made his escape to the great outdoors.

The tension was relieved a couple of days later when the chameleon was found hanging on one of the living room drapes. I often felt mother, as the result of this miniature zoo, was a little concerned about the man her daughter had married, who allowed all kinds of animals to roam freely around the house. I guess there was a side to Lawrie she wasn't familiar with, for Lawrie enjoyed the presence of these weird beasts as much as I. Jimmy, as usual, continued to spoil the baby and animals alike.

Chapter 12

ON SAFARI.

"I say old chap, do you have any idea where you are going?

COMPLETELY UNAWARE of the conditions of travel in East Africa, we decided to show the folks around the country. Obtaining a road map of the area, we planned a trip by boat from Kampala in Uganda to Mwanza in Tanzania, then drive across Tanzania to Kilimanjaro into Kenya and on to Mombasa and then back home. Everything looked great, large red lines marked the roads clearly, with lots of towns where one could stop and rest. As December marked the end of the school year, we had a six-week break in which to make the trip. We booked the steam ship across the lake and the hotels in the major parks. We felt confident we could find other places to stop if we wished. So with our three-week-old baby in the back of our Ford Cortina station wagon we set out on an adventure we were not soon to forget, in fact would never forget, as every inch of the way is still etched clearly in my mind some thirty-eight years later.

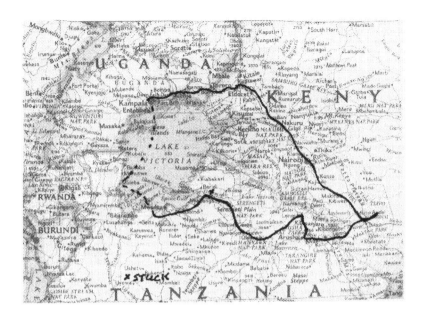

The route of our first East African safari.

The first day of our trip was just to Kampala, where next day we would embark in the African Queen. (Not really; that is what Jimmy called it.) Jimmy, who had been in Uganda long enough to experience the unorthodox driving habits of the locals, (although I often thought he would have fit in well as his driving habits were somewhat unorthodox) decided he needed a little fortification. By ten o'clock on the morning we left he was feeling no pain and was ready to tackle the world. We are sure he even kissed Yokobo goodbye and gave Marty the monkey a hug. We set off for Kampala on day one, with Douglas in the back, in his buggy, which could be removed from its wheels. Granny and Lawrie sat in the middle seat with Granddaddy in the passenger seat next to me. Feeling no pain he was singing, "If I Have Wounded Any Soul Today", as we sped past cyclists hauling their usual loads of charcoal or bananas.

We arrived safely in Kampala, booked into the Speke Hotel and spent a pleasant and restful evening. The next day we drove to the Lake Victoria steamer dock to confirm our passage to Mwanza only to find no such booking existed. Apparently a soccer team had taken priority and we had been bumped. I was set to drive around the lake but Lawrie and pop decided we would see if some arrangements couldn't be made. We could, we were told, have deck passage, which would mean we would have to sleep in deck chairs over night. Mother didn't relish the idea, especially with newborn Douglas. However, again Lawrie and pop insisted we take it and see if something else developed. So, loading our car and us onto the boat, (mother and I still whimpering about the fact our booking had been usurped), we set out on our adventure. Once we left the dock pop went to find the ships purser to see if something could be arranged for Lawrie and baby. He was successful in obtaining a cabin that would house them, plus mother. This put a different light on things as pop and I could probably stay in the lounge. Still not satisfied pop continued to pursue the possibilities of finding yet another cabin. Well, the strangest thing happened! All of a sudden we had adjoining cabins. I am not absolutely sure but I strongly suspect that pop had crossed a palm or two with silver and miraculously space had been found. More than likely at the next stop some other person had been informed his booking had been misplaced and he no longer had a cabin. Regardless of how it all worked we had a tremendous voyage and met some very interesting people. The sun set in the west as usual, (apparently no one had offered a bribe for it to do otherwise,) and shortly thereafter a beautiful full moon rose sending a golden tropical pathway across the lake, and turned the ship's wake into the yellow brick road.

That night we ate a delicious meal and later relaxed in the lounge with after dinner drinks, along with Douglas, who at that point didn't indulge in the drinks and seemed content with his milk. We slipped into conversation with an Asian family from Mwanza, which is on the southern tip of the lake in Tanzania and was our destination. They told us all about the area, what they did for a living but I think the thing that impressed pop and I was their grown daughter who, as we both admitted to each other later, was one of the most beautiful women we had ever seen.

The next morning we disembarked from the ship and started our over-land journey following the broad red lines on our East African Shell map. They did not denote super highways. Instead the roads closely resembled the well-worn trails that lead back into the hills somewhere west of my hometown of Claresholm in southern Alberta. The large dots that were accompanied by a name turned out to be three or more mud shanties, one of which was a bar. At least these people had their priorities right. So realizing that finding a decent eating establishment was out of the question we pushed on eating the snacks we had in the car. It was obvious we were not going to get a decent meal until we reached the Serengeti Lodge and this in itself was not going to be as easy as we thought.

As we reached the park entrance the road branched. The broad red line went straight ahead and our road turned into a thin black line. The one thing that can be said for Shell's East African road map was that it definitely indicated the type of road you were going to travel on once the standard was established. Now our road became two tracks through the grass, much like a railway track or the type of shortcut my father-in-law was renowned for taking. He seemed right at home and totally unconcerned. My concern was growing by the minute as we passed through a structure that was called a park gate. From here on in the road deteriorated yet further to something that resembled the tracks left by a cross-country motor rally. We picked what appeared to be the most traveled and proceeded along it. The car bounced and rocked, red murrum dust filtering through every crack in the car. Douglas, as they say, slept like a baby through all this. As we came around an acacia thicket we were greeted with a spectacular specimen of a giraffe. It appeared massive, towering what seemed like twenty feet into the air, its big dark eyes peering down at us with an expression on its face as much to say, " what the hell are you doing here"? We observed it for several minutes as it continued to enjoy its meal of tender shoots from the top of the bush. Time was passing and we had to push on. Following our selection of the best-used track, we found ourselves now entering an area that resembled a wet slough bottom and it was at this instant when mother exclaimed with excitement, "Look at the ostrich!" My eyes distracted, I slid off the track and we were stuck. We all piled out of the car. Lawrie, mom and Doug found a dry spot to sit and pop and I jacked up the car, put sticks and grass under the wheels and attempted to free it. All this was time consuming and of little use as the car mired still deeper. At this same instant a large troop of baboon appeared and the peacefully seated trio made a hasty retreat into the car, which didn't help the situation. With the afternoon passing quickly I was starting to think we may well be spending the night in our car, as our efforts to get unstuck seemed to be making little progress.

After about thirty or forty minutes, a land rover hove into view, from what appeared to be out of nowhere. The driver was a German biologist, studying the animals and vegetation of the park. He had seen us driving down the road from his home and was surprised when we didn't show up, so he eventually came out to see what had become of us. The reason the road was better traveled was because of his activities in the area. . He pulled us out and took us to his home where pop and I showered to rid ourselves of the mud. The shower was unique as it was located in the middle of a huge bougainvillea bush. After we had showered, he and his wife give us tea and snacks. I was envious of his job; it was something I would have loved to do. As time was passing very quickly and one was not allowed to drive in the park after dark we bid farewell to our rescuers and, following his directions, we again picked up the track leading to the lodge.

The road improved slightly but we now experienced places where elephants had knocked trees down over the road making it necessary to wend our way through the bush to detour around them. Eventually we arrived at the lodge just after darkness fell. Finally, we were treated to a few hundred meters of hard surface. You would think now it would be smooth sailing, oh no, for the asphalt was liberally laced with speed humps. To this day I find speed humps very disconcerting and objectionable. I couldn't believe it; some egotistical sadist must have placed them there.

Tired and hungry we found our way to the lobby housed in a large thatched roof hut, where I expected to do battle with someone who was upset by the fact that we were driving after sunset. But no, instead a friendly receptionist greeted us and we were quickly registered, our luggage taken to our rooms and the schedule for and the location of the dining room pointed out. Our rooms were airy, clean and well appointed. We showered off the newly acquired layer of dust and dressed for dinner. As we made our way to the dining room, again housed in a large thatched roof building, one had the feeling of being involved in the movie, King Salomon's Mines. The night air filled with a million calls of the animals fulfilling their role in nature and cicadas created a musical background, something one can only experience in the vast open spaces of Africa. We wended our way to the dining area, where a vast array of food was available and an abundance of waiters saw to our every need. It was easy to get a feeling of opulence and strong will power was necessary to subdue the feeling of superiority. One cannot help philosophizing that wealth has created the feeling that somehow it makes one better than those who lack it and more credence to the old saying that the love of money is the root of all evil.

The repast was bountiful and now completely sated we ambled into the lounge for a nightcap and a re-counting of the days adventures. I can remember pop turning to Lawrie and commenting that today's adventures could be a great source for some writing. As I sit here typing in my two-finger fashion, I too wonder why I'm doing this and not Lawrie, who is more intelligent and has a much better grasp of the English language. One proof of this would be to ask my English high school teacher, if she is still alive. We returned to our cabin where Douglas was sound asleep, obviously preparing for the next days travels over the rough African roads, where he could sleep some more.

Daybreak came with a sunrise that painted the sky in crimson, orange and yellow and combinations that would stretch the abilities of the most talented artist. Still dark against this backdrop was the Serengeti Plain, with huge flat top acacia trees forming magnificent silhouettes. I had longed to see this for myself ever since seeing and reading Dr. Grzimek's "Serengeti Shall Not Die", when I was attending university some five years earlier. I could now understand what drove this man and this son, the son having lost his life in a plane crash there, to devote so much time and effort to the preservation of this paradise on earth.

We motored through the park with our guide, whose knowledge abounded with information about the park's animals and plants. The gnu and wildebeest were starting their migration to greener pastures and thousands would be strung out across the plains. It resembled, I'm sure, the vast herds of buffalo that once roamed the prairies. What a pity we are such a despicable animal that we want to eradicate other species so we can make a few miserable dollars from farming. I am quite sure the economic advantage from people coming from the world over to see animals in such vast numbers as one can see in the Serengeti, would be far greater and less destructive than can be made by many of the farmers who inhabit that dry area on the prairies today. Observing this vast sanctuary I realized I must be sure to instruct my African students on the need to maintain these areas, areas they, too, thought were better being brought under cultivation. I later had the opportunity to take many of the senior boys on a field trip to parks in Uganda to show them the economic advantage of maintaining nature over agriculture. I digress, something I sometimes did in class much to the delight of my students. The unfortunate thing was I never learned in class to start with the offbeat subject and digress to the main subject area, which may have been a very valuable teaching tool. One does not realize the vast number of species that exist in these parks and unlike our parks, such as Banff, you get to see thousands of animals. Huge and seemingly ungainly giraffe, move with such elegance and grace its hard to imagine: gazelle streak across the grassland with the speed of lightning, their feet barely touching the ground: elephants and hippopotamus, whose large masses make the earth tremble as they amble along, and the majestic lions lounging under an acacia after the night's hunt. How can a big-brained, purportedly intelligent animal like ourselves be so destructive, uncaring and short sighted not to see that our own demise is built into our own stupidity if we allow such areas to disappear?

The next day we again set out with our guide to tour the park and its inhabitants. As we drove over the prairie like terrain, our guide had us stop the car and he moved silently towards a clump of grass. We watched in anticipation and then he beckoned us over. We all approached quietly to the spot where he stood, and then he parted the grass. Curled up in its small nest was a baby gazelle, its big blue watery eyes peering up at us as it lay motionless. The guide explained at that age the baby gazelle has no scent and if they remain perfectly still no predator would know they were there. He enclosed the small body again and we continued on our journey. We were rewarded later by seeing large numbers of wildebeest, Thomson gazelle, gnu, musk ox, and a pride of sated lion, having killed and eaten their fill that night. The wildlife was unending and easily visible; I have never seen anything in real life like it before or since. We must assure that African governments continue to maintain and protect such a wonder of the world.

We spent a couple of days in the Serengeti, not nearly enough to do it justice We then headed southeast, and with the excitement of the past few days and all the chatter going on in the car, we sailed by the turn off to Olduval Gorge, a site I so wanted to see, as it represented one of the birthplaces of mankind. Unfortunately by the time we realized our mistake, we were close to the end of the day and approaching our destination, Ngorongoro Crater. This huge extinct volcanic crater is ten miles across, far greater than anything that exists as volcanoes today. It forms a giant bowl filled with life and a history that has been written about by others. How I wished Douglas were ten years old rather than four weeks, that he too could have seen this. Mom and pop realized how much they had missed by not traveling to see the wonders of our world and made up for it by making two trips around the world and a number to Europe. If Lawrie and I going to Africa started something for them, then we, in a very small way, returned the legacy and support they gave us.

We traveled down into the crater by Landover, the road too steep and precipitous for an ordinary vehicle. The steep sides created a natural zoo as the animals within its bounds made little or no effort to escape its confines. As a result nature and its evolutionary magic created variations in some of the organisms, slight color changes, size and eating habits. Even this sanctuary had not escaped the invasion of the white man, as some settlers had tried to adapt it to agricultural use, but luckily had failed at the attempt. An old farmstead, its buildings in ruins still formed a wart on the surface of this unique and amazing place.

On the road again, this time to Manyara National Park and then to Amboseli National Park, which incorporates Mount Kilimanjaro. What a spectacular sight! A place where you can see snow on the equator, something the early explorers talked about but no one believed. The mountain's huge volcanic peek equaled the splendor of Japan's Mount Fiji. Here we did encounter an echo of King Solomon's Mine. As we were having dinner one evening in the lodge, in came Stewart Granger with his entourage. For those who may not know of him, he was the star of the movie and apparently was back for a visit, just for old time sake. Although this was an extra, the main highlight was still the mountain. This great volcanic peek, thousands of feet high, snow covered and as stated situated almost smack dab on the equator. In the mountain's shadow dwelt the Masai, a tribe of people who, unlike the Bantu are tall and wiry. They are herdsman, maintaining large herds of cattle, which are not only a source of food but are the means of exchange like our money. They inhabit small villages that consist of groups of houses inside an acacia brush coral, called a boma. Although once suspicious of strangers, they now wheel and deal with the tourists, selling spears, shields, head dresses and decorated gourds. Other than this exchange of goods for money, now needed in the modern African society, they live much as they always have; a proud and self-assured people. Their life style, although interesting, is not one I would wish to emulate. The houses are composed of mud and cow manure, which prevents the termites from destroying them, their roofs made of cowhides. The combination tends to give off an odor that would take some getting use to. The interior of the boma is well kept and swept clean of the cow dung deposited by the herd during the night. The cattle were kept inside at night to protect them from the wild predators. During the day the men and young boys of the village herd them from one area to another, assuring a constant source of good grazing. At one time a boy was expected to kill a lion with his spear as one stage of gaining manhood. He would also at this stage start to gather together a cattle herd of his own, and when he married the bride's family was expected to give him cattle as part of the dowry. This, like most African societies and like our own not so many years earlier, was male oriented and dominated.

From here our travels took us to Arusha and on to Tsavo in Kenya, a dry more desert-like region, and the area where the story involving "The Man Eaters Of Tsavo" occurred during the building of the East African Railway. Lions still roam the area but there have been few if any incidences of them eating men since that time. We stayed in the park that night and, like all beds in the lodges in East Africa they were covered with mosquito netting. In most cases it was almost unnecessary and so we took it in our nonchalant stride. We retired to bed, but during the night pop had to get up for a trip to the bathroom. He turned on the light and before you could blink the netting was covered with insects of all shapes, colors and sizes. Mother, whose tolerance to insects was about the same as most peoples for snakes, sat bolt upright, abruptly screaming and shouting, while at the same time beating the netting with her hand. This sent the insects into a frenzied cloud, causing a flutter and humming that rivaled mother's shrill shouts. Pop, having missed most of this, returned to receive a scolding better than many he had encountered during his married life. Getting the lights off seemed to settle things down, including mother. The insects out of sight and out of mind made her less hysterical. Pop was again snoring before the rest of us could regain sleep, with the exception of Douglas.

In Tsavo, we were shown a tamed rhinoceros, with which pop had his picture taken. This was sent back to the grand children in Canada, with the note that it had taken him all day to tame this beast to the point where he could have his picture taken with it. This was the type of thing pop, or granddaddy as he was affectionately known, was renowned for among the grandkids. The time spent in Tsavo brought to an end this, our first, East African tour of some of the game parks and, as time was running out, we were unable to go to Mombasa, so from Tsavo we motored on paved highway back to Jinja, and Busoga College, via Nairobi.

Douglas, having bumped his way across a vast expanse of East Africa in a state of slumber, now tossed and turned as the car glided along the smooth asphalt. How weird can a kid get? The Kergan's holiday time was coming to a close once we arrived back home, with only a few days relaxing left before the next stage of their journey. We had enjoyed their company in the paradise we now called home.

Chapter 13

SETTLING IN TO UGANDAN LIFE

Me! Wear shorts?

AFTER A fantastic trip with Lawrie's mom and dad, they having flown on to Australia and New Zealand, we settled in for another term of school. I was very much looking forward to this new term as I now had my feet wet in the British system and a much better handle on the courses I was to teach. I felt much better having traveled during the autumn and Christmas breaks around Uganda and now through parts of East Africa. I felt, whether true or not, that I had some understanding of the area from which my students came. I no longer had to try and imagine the area when they were describing their homes. You realized how sincere and conscientious these boys were about school and their studies, when you saw the background from which they came and the opportunity an education gave them; no cost or sacrifice was too high. Now I knew why these boys would study far into the night past lights out. .

Being the electrical master, I was asked by the headmaster if it was possible to install time switches in all the dormitories, so the lights would shut off at eleven o'clock.

I indicated it wouldn't be a problem. The reason for this was the headmaster felt a great many of the boys were not getting adequate sleep as they would turn the lights back on to study after the duty master had made his rounds. The time switches were to prevent this from happening. During the autumn holiday period I fulfilled this task. That first night after their return, a cacophony of noise arose from the dorms when the lights, except those in the toilet areas, all went off. This created a great many questions next day but apparently at assembly the situation was explained. To prevent the boys getting too upset, I believe they were told it was to conserve electricity and cut costs. This was a valid reason and apparently was accepted at face value. However, the boys were not to be deterred: after that they either studied in the bathrooms or used flashlights. Could you possibly imagine a North American student going to such extremes? But to them an education was vital.

Although they had a well-rounded day, with sports activities and various societies, their main concern was gleaning and storing information to assure their school life ended in success. The school term was divided into three sections and there was a one-day-break half way through each term. This was firmly established and the only thing that would result in other days off was if the water pump at the bottom of the hill broke down. My neighbor Doug Turner was the water master and under his watchful eye, it generally ran without interruption. But like any mechanical devise it would sometimes give up the ghost. If the problem was serious it could well mean the boys would be sent home, a disaster as far as the students were concerned, as it meant the loss of class time and an added expense of traveling home and back again. The African students were driven by the goals of gaining professional status, an important government position and wealth. This was all supported by the fact that Dr. Obote, the president, was an old boy of the school.

The boys minds weren't always on school work for as young men they became horny, and most of them were young men, so on occasion one or two would sneak down to a small village below the hill after lights out and indulge in a few drinks of local beer and a romp in the hay with a girl. Sex was not considered bad in their eyes, only in those of their white straight-laced teachers. In most cases none would be any the wiser, the exception being the few who contracted a venereal disease and had to make a trip to the school nurse. This was not a pleasant condition as a trip to the nurse, (Naomi by name and who was still alive at the time of writing,) was by the boys considered worse than the disease. Naomi was an older lady and very religious, and she was not beyond giving them a horrendous lecture along with not too gentle a treatment. They were also reported to the headmaster and if the offense occurred more than a couple of times the culprit could see an end to his school career. I think Daniel's advice to early offenders would be that it wasn't worth losing your head over a piece of tail, as he sentenced them to heavy duty physical labor by way of punishment. The advice was often taken to heart and in today's Africa an absolute necessity, for now I wonder if their school careers may well be ended not by disciplinary action but by death as AIDS has become so widespread.

Sports were a big part of their school life but, interestingly enough, so was drama. The boys loved to be involved in plays of all descriptions. All parts both male and female were played by boys, who had no qualms about dressing up in girl's clothing. They had the added advantage of not growing vast amounts of body hair like their less evolved white counterparts. They certainly had no need for Neat to give them beautifully smooth legs. With great enthusiasm and voices raised to a falsetto they performed their roles admirably. If any affection was to be shown they threw themselves into it with gusto. No thoughts of homosexuality entered any of their heads. It is commonplace to see men holding hands strolling down the road; it gives them a feeling of bonding, nothing sexual. Thus, they threw themselves into their parts with such an exuberant manner that the audience was soon involved, including us overly prudish white types.

This again points out the need for more people to travel and see how different people live. I am sure that racial and cultural barriers would certainly be lessened. The cultural differences were certainly brought home to us when we were invited to one of the boy's homes. A senior student, Paul Wangola, took Lawrie and I to his village and as we drove up the whole village was there to greet us with drums and dancing. They led us into the center of their small mud hut community, where we were honored and welcomed with a great deal of hand shaking and Ugandan smiles. Apparently such a greeting was only given to people of prominence, I accepted the prominence having never received it before or since.

Once in the compound we were seated at the only table in the place and brought a huge plate of chicken and various vegetables, along with tea, and chapatis (a pancake like bread). We both felt a little guilty, as I am sure they didn't eat that well all the time. The food was superbly prepared on open charcoal fires and served on plates in our case but most ate from a section of banana leaf, which would have suited us just fine. While we ate, some of the girls sang and the men danced to the rhythmic beat of the drumming, supplied by a small group all playing different sized drums. The main course finished, we were served a type of curdled milk dessert. As I dislike anything that resembles curdled milk, I found it more than I wanted to experience even if it was the true Ugandan cuisine. However for fear of offending both Lawrie and I sampled the bowl of whitish-green congealed material. It tasted as I suspected, like badly spoiled milk with the texture of worm slime. It was all I could do to prevent myself from revisiting the first course.

We begged off further indulgence, by explaining that it was difficult for us to enjoy, as we had never experienced a similar taste before. This was accepted as an excuse for our reluctance to finish the bowl. Now I know why some people dislike the things I like, we must taste things differently. Later we found out that in many cases the milk is prematurely soured with cow urine, this knowledge, of course would have made it even more delightful for us.

After our meal we had a chance to speak with other members of the group either directly in English or through our student interpreter. We found out that all pitched in, including the men, to cultivate the banana trees, the cassava, (the plant from which we obtain tapioca), along with peanuts, sweet potatoes and other leafy plants with which I was unfamiliar. The water was hauled from a stream over a quarter of a mile away by the women. As mentioned earlier, the women did most of the work. It reminds me of the story that was told about North American natives. Before the white man came the men hunted all day, the women did all the work and they paid no income tax and the white man thought he could improve on that. We didn't improve on it but the Ugandan men obviously did, as they didn't have to hunt unless they really felt the urge and they still did only marginal amounts of the gardening and household chores.

The other interesting aspect of the village was the witch doctor, who in this case was a woman, a rare situation. She had a mud hut where she practices her trade. The church area, for want of a better description, consisted of a larger outer room, where groups could meet and a small inner sanctum, which resembled a confessional. Here she would cast spells both good and bad, remove spells when needed and do incantations to assure good crops, improve a couple's fertility and a number of other functions. She obviously had a great deal of power and respect. We may well consider this all very silly and pagan but having experienced one situation involving one of the students, I don't dismiss it out of hand.

One day the house prefect came to the door to tell me that a student, who's name I have unfortunately forgotten, was lying on his bed as though in death. This seemed serious so I quickly went to see. By the time I arrived he had come out of this state and seemed quite normal. I told the boys to call me immediately, day or night if this occurred again. One afternoon a student came racing to my door to tell me that the boy had again gone into this coma-like state. I rushed to the house and found him on the floor. He was cool and clammy, breathing slowly but rhythmically but otherwise lifeless. I thought this was something more serious than the school nurse could handle so I got my car, placed the student in it and rushed him to the doctor in Jinja. Twenty minutes had passed when we arrived at the doctor's office and he was still out like a light. He was immediately taken into the doctor's surgery, where he was examined for vital signs. The eye's irises closed when exposed to light, his knee jerked when hit with the rubber hammer, heart rate and respiration were fine, but he was cold and limp. Finally he started to stir and his eyes opened wide, he looked puzzled by the fact he was in strange surroundings. The doctor assured him he was okay and he soon became his normal self. The doctor was stymied by what he had seen and reported that all body functions were normal, other than this coma like state.

I took the boy back to the school and reported the situation to the headmaster. When he heard the story, he immediately sent for the boy, and he told him he would be sent home and that he was to get the spell removed. Why he had a spell on him I never did learn, but I would have loved to know the details. A few weeks later the boy returned and was never affected by the condition again. Was it a spell, a type of hypnotism, a condition brought on by stress? I'll never know. However, listening and watching the old witch doctor, I couldn't help wonder what powers she may have had, that we, with all our modern medicine fail to comprehend.

Our visit to the village again reinforced how little knowledge we have of others in our world and how cocksure we are in the western world, that we are the only ones who have it right. It is obvious that racial prejudice will be with us for a long time to come and it is not a one sided thing.

Chapter 14

SOME BIZARRE THINGS
THAT HAPPENED

*Oh give me a home where the python roam
and the insects tickle your fancy.*

THE STUDENTS were always looking for a cause to have a celebration, and the occasional celebration in the dormitory was called a komolo. This involved some dancing, drumming, the drinking of a milk and sugar laden tea and the eating of cakes, usually supplied by the wives of the house-master and the deputy house-master, namely Lawrie Peters and Mary Turner. Brewer House's deputy housemaster was Doug Turner, an older man from Derbyshire in England. He and Mary had three children, Elizabeth, better known as Liz, and a son John. The elder daughter Jennifer had stayed in England to work. Doug, as previously mentioned, was master in charge of the water pump. He was also the teacher of industrial arts, which fortunately meant he was mechanically oriented. The whole family was a jolly, fun loving lot and the boys had a great deal of respect for him as well as a lot of seductive looks for his daughter. Doug, being my deputy, was a big help for this meant I now had someone to look after the religious aspect of the house, which he did willing. He, being older, became the mzee, (wise elder) and the boys confided in him readily.

The boys announced they were going to have a komolo and naturally we were all invited, especially Liz. The Turners came to our house first and we visited before going to the dormitory. As time came to go over to the dormitory, we set out, flashlights in hand. We started across the hundred yards of lawn that separated the two buildings, but what we weren't aware of was the fact that a mass of army ants had decided to cross the lawn on a diagonal path to ours. Army ants are ferocious little critters, having been known to eat every thing in their path including frogs, snakes and small animals. Nothing diverted these single-minded insects from their set course of travel, including six determined mzungus (white men). I was leading the group, followed almost immediately by Doug. Without realizing it I stepped into the ant's pathway. With lightning speed they were climbing my legs. No sooner had I gone into my involuntary war dance than Doug began to follow suit. The others, a little further behind and not quite sure what was going on, held back just out of range of Attila and his marauding army. By this time they had proceeded well up on our bodies and were biting Doug and I with their razor sharp mandibles. Realizing we had a problem we shouted to the others not to come any closer. John spotted the river of ants with his flashlight and directed the ladies to step over it and continue to the dormitory. Doug and I went running, jumping, slapping and gyrating to Brewer House in record time where we ran into the toilet area, stripped off our clothes, beating these little black adversaries to death as the survivors continued to try and kill with sharp painful bites, these bouncing mountains of white blubber. When we exited the bathroom looking rather disheveled we were met with huge grins on the faces of the boys, they having been told by the members of our entourage what had happened. Now that we were not being eaten alive by our little black tormentors, I could also start to appreciate the ridiculous sight Doug and I must have made, the two dauntless leaders leading their band, turned into cartoon characters by organisms no more than a half an inch long.

This wasn't the only incident involving insects and myself that took on comic like qualities. The other that comes to mind was the day the Plumtrees, a wonderful missionary couple who had spent years on the hill, came to me to see if I could remove a bees nest housed in the roof of their veranda. This seemed like a good opportunity to obtain some bees for a beehive. I busily set to making a hive into which the bees would be placed once I had retrieved them from the roof. I decked myself out with a netted hood, gloves and rubber boots. Feeling adequately equipped for the task, I began removing some of the ceiling panels in the veranda. All was going well, as the bees were not too concerned about this intrusion until I got closer to the comb. At this point, as though they had been lying in ambush, they streamed out of every nook and cranny and swarmed over their attacker, much in the same way the Indian war party swept down on the wagon train in a B western.

Being good at nooks and crannies, they managed to find their way under my clothing. The first few stings alerted me to the fact that my armor left a lot to be desired. I decided on a speedy retreat to the closest dormitory, stripped down to my under pants and beat the little buggers to death, however not before they managed to sting me several more times. Luckily my parents raised bees and I had developed some immunity to their venom. Undaunted I returned home and doubled up on the clothing and closed off the arms and legs with some large rubber bands. Now resembling an alien from an old Star Trek show, I returned to the war zone. The Plumtrees, along with their son and mine were cowering inside the house, held captive by the bees, which were still in a high state of agitation. Again I attacked, again they counter attacked and yet again they somehow managed to infiltrate my defenses and put me on the run. Taking refuge in the dormitory and again being stung several more times, I now realized this was all out war and the need to employ different weapons became evident.

Having now armed myself with a can of gasoline and a medieval flaming torch I launched a counter attack of my own. As they swooped out I engulfed them in the flames, sending them spiraling to the ground like World War 1 biplanes. However, much like the Chinese army, they kept coming in such numbers I could not beat them back. Nimbly jumping from the stepladder I again made for the dorm. This time bearing my torch and not looking exactly where I was going, I kicked over and set fire to my small container of gasoline. Now I was fleeing from two foes, the enraged bees and a trail of fire, out-sprinting both. Still the bees got in their licks and managed a few more counter punches. Thinking of Mad Dogs and Englishmen that in this case was just a mad Canadian Englishman (no dogs), these bees were too damn smart for me. I attacked again with a new torch and gasoline supply. This simple operation had now dragged into a two or more hour episode. Armed with a long hoe I pulled down the rest of the ceiling tiles containing the nest, now I finally had my enemy in the open. I waved and lunged with my torch, like a knight of old, burning and pillaging the bee village. As the smoke cleared I could see I had won the war and although my prize lay in smoldering ruins on the ground I felt an upsurge of power, much as the Romans may have felt at the sacking Carthage.The bees, cleaned up in more ways than one, and the ceiling tiles replaced I went home feeling only mild soreness from the numerous wounds inflicted on me by my adversaries.

As mentioned earlier I was appointed electricity master and I performed many tasks that may well have landed me in serious trouble here in Canada. One such incident involved a visit to a neighboring school, where our friend Ax Benzon taught. Lawrie and I were invited for supper and luckily just as all the cooking was completed the power went off in half the school. Not too concerned as it was the electrical master's job to contact the Uganda Electrical Board, we assumed it would be on soon. Our group settled in for a leisurely candle lit meal, enjoying the ambiance created by the flickering light. The meal finished we retired to the living room for coffee, which the houseboy had managed to brew, more than likely on his charcoal stove. We were served coffee, followed by a few drinks. The candles, by now getting close to the end of their life expectancy, made our anxiety grow. Our attitudes were now changing from; "isn't this fun", to "this is getting ridiculous". The fact the electricity master's lights were on along with the other half of the school made it obvious a master fuse had blown at the transformer. The idea occurred to me that we should change fuses with those who had been enjoying power. This doubly appealed to us as the electricity master was among those still enjoying electrical power. We drove Axel's car to the transformer pole and as luck would have it we could reach the big pot fuses by standing on its roof. Borrowing a flashlight from a passing teacher I found the faulty fuse and replaced it with the other. Having switched the fuses we went back to a well-lit house to enjoy the rest of the evening. Later we found out we had plunged the headmaster into darkness just as he was getting out of the bath. It is surprising what necessity will do, as in the case of the smashed windows by Mr. Carlson, for in less than an hour the whole school was once again enjoying the benefits of electrical service.

An incident that caught the attention of the whole school was the day an eleven-foot python came to call. All the boys gathered around the area where the python lay curled up in a thicket. Upon encountering the scene I felt initially that the best thing to do was to try and get the snake to move on to another out of the way place. The better thing to do in retrospect was to leave it alone and it would have gone away of its own volition. However, the boys were sure it was about to do someone harm, so as I was the biology teacher, it was suggested by some idiot, (it may even have been me), that the reptile be disposed of in some manner.

My first attempt was to try and dislodge the snake and have it slither off out of sight and out of mind. This however did not work so a second plan was needed. I secured a length of rope and a long stick. I fashioned a lariat out of the rope and with the stick I attempted to get the snake to raise its head. Several attempts were made to no avail. One boy commented that someone was about to die, this I found extremely reassuring. At about this time Doug Turner arrived on the scene with a stout hoe handle from his workshop. Two or three more attempts were made and success was achieved as the noose tightened around the slender neck. As I pulled on the rope the snake dug in its heels, for a snake a difficult task. Doug and a couple of other teachers joined in the pull and gradually the reptile relented and was pulled into the open. Lucky for us it didn't lunge forward or I'm sure panic would have set in which would have given the snake a second chance at freedom. The natural tendency was for the animal to pull back and so with several quick blows on the head it was quickly dispatched. The excitement over, the boys dispersed and I was left with the dead snake. Although snakeskin shoes did not seem to befit my nature, I did decide I would skin it and have the hide tanned. I did end up with a couple of nice handbags, which by the way were for Lawrie not me, and several wallets, which made interesting Christmas gifts for the family back home in Canada.

Although many interesting incidents occurred, the last two I will tell involved our monkey. One that I will relate is the story, as told by Mike Leigh, the history teacher, of our monkey on a visit to his class. Marty had the whole school compound in which to roam and did. Mike taught history from the white man's point of view, as was necessary if the students were to pass their Cambridge O and A level examinations. Mike was well respected by the boys as an extremely competent teacher in his field as well as one that made history an enjoyable adventure through time. In the corner of each classroom was a cupboard in which books, maps and the like where kept. One day while Mike was teaching, Marty sauntered into the room through an open window, made his way to the top of the cupboard and proceeded to look as though he had come to inspect the proceedings. After listening for a period of time, Marty's head drooped, his eyes closed and he appeared to doze off. He assumed the pose for quite a long period of time then stood up, stretched, yawned and strode out. This prompted some laughter in the classroom and a comment by Mike to me later, in the telling that he felt he had better start reviewing his lessons for the interest factor.

The second story involved the wife of Ossie Butler, the English teacher who had made the comment about the student working like a nigger. Beryl and Ossie had a large family consisting of two sons and a daughter of their own, plus two adopted sons. Beryl very seldom received a lot of time to herself but one beautiful sunny day she decided to relax in their front yard under the shade of a large eucalyptus tree. Feeling the heat of the sun she began to feel a little sleepy and she had drifted of into the gray area between consciousness and sleep. Totally relaxed she lay in her reclining deck chair totally enjoying her solitude. Suddenly something cold and clammy landed on her shoulder. Small cold hands and feet dug into her shoulder to withstand her sudden movement, and bristly hair rubbed against her face. Her heart was doing triple time as surprise and fear careened through her body and she leaped from her chair with agility she didn't realize she possessed, giving a blood-curdling scream. She wildly slapped at the intruder, who by now had leaped to the ground. In that first split second she was sure a snake lurking in the branches above had landed on her, bent on doing her no good. Then she spotted Marty, sitting just out of range of any other gyrations that might occur, his two large black eyes full of surprise equal to her own She recognized Marty immediately and realized he had just dropped in for a social visit on his way home from one of his many adventures.

Chapter 15

THE COAST

Paradise regained

I F YOU spend time in East Africa, it is absolutely essential that you go to the coastal regions of Kenya, for it is an area of the world like no other. We arrived in Mombasa, a town initially started by Arab traders, fortified by the Portuguese with Fort Jesus, and later taken over by the British, as so many things were. Mombasa is an extremely unique place, a place where you can obtain almost anything you want, both legal and illegal. It is a mixture of African, Arab, Asian and European. For variety and uniqueness it has few rivals, a place that captures your fascination and curiosity. As you drive into the main street area you are greeted by a grand archway resembling two elephant tusks, a debatable tribute to the massive ivory trade that went on here. Even in those days the animals seemed to be able to reproduce and maintain their status quo. Then came the white man and his insatiable need to control, conquer and change a system that had been in place and working for the native people for thousands of years. This succession is inevitable, so I guess we shouldn't be surprised when what we feel is now ours, will be challenged by peoples from lands far more crowded than our own. As the old saying suggests, "what goes around comes around."

If and when you travel you cannot help but be educated by what you see, and the more you learn the better teacher of others you will become. Although, as I said earlier, I never considered myself a great teacher, I certainly became a better one for having had so many great experiences. Even if one's ability to impart subject material didn't improve, your understanding of people and why they think the way they do is definitely increased, although one really never becomes an expert. When I first joined C.I.D.A, we were known as experts, something I found very questionable, especially in light of the definition I gave earlier. Thus when our title became advisors, I found it much more to my liking.

Mombasa, situated on the Indian Ocean with its palm trees and sandy beaches, immediately made me feel neither an expert nor an advisor but rather one of the luckiest people in the world to have the opportunity to soak up the history, the human mosaic and the magnificent scenery. As well as being a city of mixed nationalities, it is also a mixture of sights and smells. The intermingling of cultural smells, African charcoal and steamed banana, Asian curry, Arab tobacco and coffee and European food and industry, fills the air. The smells of luxury mixed with the smells of poverty. The stores are filled to over flowing with all types of mystical and ornate articles. You feel much as Ali Baba did when he found himself inside the cave of the forty thieves. The main difference is the present owners were more than anxious to sell you the items and unlike here in Canada, nothing has a set price, only a starting point for the haggling. These merchants enjoy their business no end and the sport of haggling is a major part of that enjoyment. From this you realize how boring, sterile and inhuman a place like Wal Mart is, to name only one example. The fun of merchandising is lost in a big dollar sign.

Photographs Of Places In The Mombasa Area

The elephant tusks on Main Street   A typical downtown street

Fort Jesus from the ocean   Fort Jesus from land side

Ruins at Gedi

The amazing thing is how trusting these people are, contrary to our conception that these traders are only thieves in merchants clothing. Any merchant in East Africa would except your personal cheque for any item you wished to purchase, or so it was in the early nineteen seventies. In our society, then and now, we have an innate distrust of everyone, which is a good thing, or many lawyers may find themselves short of work. How easy it is to switch tracks or even become derailed as your thoughts or actions lead from one thing to another. Here I have gone from the beauties of Mombasa to an attack on our society, but digression and cynicism becomes more evident in my life as I get older, for things seemed so much simpler and straightforward in my youth. One thing that is relevant is that the times we spent in Africa were some of the most carefree yet exhilarating times of our lives and I know Lawrie would agree.

The coast provided memories that were exciting and fascinating and remain etched in our minds forever. The beautiful scenery and magnificent coral reefs were near the top of the list. North of Mombasa was the small town of Malindi with expansive white sandy beaches, palm trees and a magnificent coral reef with species of sea life far too numerous to mention. The reef was easily accessible by native dugout, and for a few shillings you could hire a native guide who would row you out to an area sheltered by an outer reef. Here you could slip over the edge of the dugout and with snorkel and goggles, float aimlessly on the surface and peer down several feet to see the colorful corals and thousands of fish dressed in their flowing and brilliant colors. The whole scene unfolded like a well-choreographed Broadway musical. All the movement was eloquent and serene, yet each species was searching out a food source and they in turn were keeping a wary eye for fear of becoming lunch themselves. Floating across this underwater stage you would suddenly come to the edge and the same fear as gripped the ancient mariners of falling off the edge of the earth would come over you. Quickly turning you would stroke your way back into the hypnotic world of the reef. The mzungus, who had spent the day snorkeling over the reef stood out among all the others, as they had the appearance of a two layer Neapolitan ice cream, their backs a bright pink and their front white. The sunburn was well worth the agony for the delight we had received obtaining it.

Here you could enjoy the life of the idle, if not so rich, with all the luxuries and services. Lawrie and I could enjoy some of the nightlife, while Douglas was in the capable hands of a native babysitter. Our babysitter was one of the most beautiful women you could imagine and I felt envious of our son whom we left in her care, but it meant we could go to the local hotel and enjoy a great evening of dining on lobster and other assorted sea foods plus dancing to the music of the day. Afterwards a moonlight stroll back along the beach to our own Shangri-La, a twelve by twelve plywood sided tent, which is all that was needed in such an idyllic place.

Besides the beauty is the history. Now several miles inland is the once coastal Arab community of Gedi. Monkeys, birds and other forms of life you are not glad to encounter, now inhabit the ruins which are still very visible among the trees that form a huge green canopy over them. The layout resembles the old Greek cities, with the town square, army barracks, administration center and surrounding dwellings. The amazing thing is the fact that in a thousand years the coral reef had added to the land mass so that now as mentioned it was several miles from the ocean. The whole substratum is limestone, the remains of the coral that flourished and formed the home for millions of sea organisms. The entire region serves as a laboratory for the anthropologist, historian, geologist and biologist, plus an area of extreme fascination for the modern tourist.

Chapter 16

THE KERGAN'S RETURN TO AFRICA

Never give your in-laws free accommodation.

JIMMY AND Chrissy Kergan returned to Uganda in nineteen seventy shortly after our second son Colin was born. Colin has returned to Uganda, at the time of writing, for a holiday to visit the land of his birth, thirty-four years later. Lawrie's mother always said she was going to be present at the birth of her grandchildren and she was more or less as good as her word. Having visited us after Doug's birth they were back for their second tour. It was not difficult to get them back after such an enjoyable first trip. This time we did plan to visit Mombasa, as well as the northern region of Uganda, known as the Karamoja.

Our visit to the coast impressed them immensely for the reason I mentioned earlier. The only thing that mother found upsetting was being presented with a couple of octopuses. While I was on the beach, a fellow came along selling the octopus. As I didn't have money on me I sent him to our cabin. Unfortunately mother was the only one around at the time. When the fellow presented the octopus to her she went into a series of grotesque gestures, chasing the poor fellow away.

Jimmy and Chrissie Kergan getting into the African spirit.

He returned to me looking a little shaken, explaining that "memsab was karli sana", which meant angry and miserable. As a result I returned to the cabin with him and paid him and he went away much happier. I tried cooking the octopus (I had tried and liked octopus at a seafood buffet in Vancouver), however my method of preparation was unsuccessful and when we attempted to eat it, the meat was rubbery and ricocheted around our mouths like a ball in a squash court. We did all the things you did at the coast and returned to Uganda.

Instead of returning directly home we turned north to a region that was considered primitive by other Ugandans. We had some students from this region and you could not tell them from the rest. Thus even in this area the elementary schools turned out some excellent products. However the general rule was that, like the Masai, they did not ape the way of the westerner but lived much as they had for centuries. This meant that they wore little or no clothing and lived in villages not too different from that of the Masai. Their life centered on their cattle herd, which was one of their main sources of food, although it wasn't the meat from the animal they wanted. Instead they would tie a rope around the animal's neck tight enough to make the veins stand out. Then with a bow and arrow, would shoot the animal in the neck to puncture the vein but not do a lot of injury to the animal itself. They would collect the blood from the wound in a gourd and mix it with the milk. Then, while eating a chapati they would drink the blood-milk mixture. This of course was an excellent source of protein.

Jimmy and I watched this exercise in one of their villages and turned down the opportunity to take part in the afternoon tea break. It must have been nutritious as they all looked healthy and muscular. The other aspect that made Jimmy and I a little gun shy was the fact that this seemed to be the same time that the flies also stopped for lunch and they would crawl all over the faces of the individuals as they ate. It nearly drove us insane as the flies even checked us out to make sure we didn't have any morsels for them. To help keep them at bay we lit up cigarettes and this in turn created a stampede among the inhabitants as they enjoyed smoking as much or more than lunch. We were soon depleted of cigarettes and blue smoke was drifting up to the sky all over the compound, much to the chagrin of the flies.

Jimmy chatting with village inhabitants Jimmy leaving compound

After leaving the village we drove up the road and encountered men tending their herds and women doing women's chores. We stopped to take a picture of a man leaning on a spear, a small three-legged stool at his feet and his cape flying about his waist in the wind. He was totally unconcerned about the resulting display of his "private" parts. Body parts were body parts so what in hell is all the fuss about. However, it wasn't his sex organ display that captured our attention but rather a sheet of metal, about three inches by six inches, probably from a tin can, that hung from a wire that went through a piercing in the septum between his nostrils. This was, I believe, there to help keep the flies away much like a cow's tail. The fact the wind was churning it about, made my nose hurt just to watch it.

We also stopped to take the picture of a lady whose neck was surrounded by bead necklaces. These were piled one on top the other so she could not lower her chin onto her chest. This we discovered was a symbol of prestige for the more necklaces you had the more important you were in the hierarchy of the village's women. It was interesting to note that she appeared to have a scar on her stomach region that may have resulted from an appendix operation or a caesarean birth. However, it did indicate that some medical services were available to them, but on the whole, other more "civilized" Ugandans treated them as second-class citizens. This was also illustrated by the fact that the Ugandan army of the time reportedly used them as target practice. Man, regardless of creed, color or nationality can be a brutal and sadistic monster.

We motored to the extreme northern end of Uganda next to the Sudan boarder, to Kidepo National Park. At the park lodge was a so-called "tame" ostrich, but you didn't want to get too close to her, as she might well peck you or give you a swift kick with one of her feet. Although we took pictures, Granddaddy didn't claim to have tamed her like he did the rhinoceros in Tsavo. This park had vast numbers of what are known as reticulated giraffe, as opposed to the Masai giraffe, found in the Serengetti, the differences being that the reticulated variety was a little smaller and their patterns were not blotches, but rather well defined squares. Along with this wonderful beast were many of the other animals we encountered in other parks, plus the well-known tsetse fly. They are the carriers of elephantiasis, although only a very small percentage carried it. This was fortunate as we did get bitten, and I mean bitten! I swear to god they had pliers in their pockets with which they nipped you, or that is what it felt like. As you left the tsetse fly area, a man with a net would examine your car, inside and out to assure you didn't take any with you to another area. The tsetse fly is a very lazy character and refuses to fly for any long distance but is not averse to hitching a ride on or in your vehicle.

The Karamoja is totally different to the rest of Uganda, as mentioned, in population and terrain. The region is very dessert-like and harsh with a great many igneous intrusions, like the Devil's Tower in Wyoming. Thank God I wasn't born a Karamojan! We turned south to return to the lush countryside around Busoga College and thanked our lucky stars we weren't assigned to a school in that northern region, although it may well have proven very interesting.

People of the Karamoja

Chapter 17

BEAVER AND HIS RELATIVES

Well I'll be a monkey's uncle.

B EAVER WAS a very young chimpanzee and was owned by a bachelor fellow living near Masindi who was a friend of a Canadian couple we knew, Norm Erickson and his wife Darlene. Beaverbrook was the chimp's full name and when you got close to the animal you realized he had no trouble being man's cousin. They are as close to being human as you can get, without being human. We arranged to stay at Beaver's owners place for a few days as he had a small house he rented out and it was close to a forest where chimpanzees lived. As a family we traveled out to the forest in hopes of seeing the chimps in their natural habitat but were unsuccessful except for a black flash moving through the canopy of the forest. Disappointed, we drove back to our cabin, not paying a great deal of attention to the surroundings. As I drove along I noticed a person sitting beside the road a couple of hundred yards ahead. A person sitting beside the road was not an uncommon sight. However as we came closer I realized it was a big old male chimp. I shouted at Lawrie and Doug, now around four, "look it's a chimpanzee". I pulled the car to a stop and we were able to watch him scamper into the surrounding brush too quickly for me to get a picture. That was the only chimpanzee we ever saw in the wild.

Back at the house we did have Beaver to observe and with which to interact. It is unbelievable how smart he was. Douglas thought he would make a great playmate but Beaver was a bit of a bully. Until Douglas smartened up, Beaver would coax him away from the house and then he would jump on him and wrestle him to the ground, pulling Doug's hair. This would immediately make Doug howl and I would have to run and rescue him. Beaver didn't restrict his attention only to Doug. Colin, who was only months old and was being fed from a bottle also caught Beaver's attention. His owner also gave beaver, still very young, milk now and then in a bottle. While Colin was being fed Beaver came up and sat beside him, he watched for a moment and I managed to capture this cozy picture on film. As Beaver watched, his rounded muzzle started to elongate until it resembled the end of a fire hose. His mouth was just a small hole just the right size to fit around a nipple. He sat, his face elongated looking at the bottle on which Colin was sucking, his eyes saying, "come on, its my turn!" Then without warning he leaned over and thumped Colin in the chest.

Beaver and Colin minutes before Colin was given his bottle

Colin spat out the bottle followed by a rush of air, his face crinkled up, his eyes filled with tears and he let out a bellow that even startled Beaver. Lawrie quickly cradled Colin in her arms and settled him down, once again introducing the bottle to his mouth. The one thing we found with our children was that the presence of food always had a settling effect. Beaver was hustled off and in future Colin was fed when Beaver was nowhere in sight.

Both the boys found Beaver to be a robust and overpowering playmate so it was left to me to entertain him. This I did mainly by playing hide and seek or catch me if you can. On one catch me if you can game I chased him around the house and through the front door. At this point I was gaining ground. Beaver nipped smartly out through some French doors at the rear with me in hot pursuit. Ambling along on all fours he passed through the doors spun on his heels and with his long arms grabbed the door fronts and slammed them shut in my face just as I arrived. You could see the wheels turning in his mind as he did it. Pretty intelligent for a dumb animal! He got me on that one but to prove I was just as smart as any stupid ape, I retraced my steps and hid on him behind a large bush. I knew his curiosity would get the better of him sooner or later and sure enough, it wasn't long before he came to find me. I let him just get past the bush and then with a blood curdling scream I lunged out from my hiding place. He jumped four feet in the air and turned to face me on the way down. He jumped to one side as I made a grab for him. Still jumping up and down, his teeth showing but not in anger, he beat his chest and made a high pitch screeching noise. He turned and ambled away and the game was on once more. I laughed and thought, "Well done, you finally out-smarted him". It made me feel good anyway. When I told Lawrie, I think it confirmed her belief that I did have a modicum of intelligence.

The other thing that made Beaver so human like was his ability to laugh. I would place him on my lap and rub his back; he would lean back in ecstasy. As I continued to scratch his neck and ears, his eyes would close in a state of complete relaxation. Finally I would tickle him under the chin and he would break into gales of laughter. He was so human that if you had your eyes closed and he wasn't so hairy you could well imagine him to be a little child.

I often feel we are too busy measuring how clever we are to notice or realize how clever other animals are that share our planet. One time when I had a senior class from Busoga College out on a field trip, we stopped at the Entebbe zoo. Surprising as it may be, most of the boys had never seen many of the animals that occupy their land. Few if any had seen a chimpanzee. In one rather bleak cage was a large male chimp, looking very bored, not surprising considering the conditions. At the back of the cage was a concrete bench on which he was lounging. Near the front was his water basin and food dish. This organism that looked so much like us fascinated the boys. They all crowded around the cage examining the chimp and commenting on its appearance. The chimp ignored them for the longest time and then he rolled off the bench and in a flash was across the cage. Before anyone could move, his hand hit the water in the dish and he sent a huge spray out over the onlookers. You could see the amusement spread across his face as he sauntered back to his resting place. Soon he was rolling around doing somersaults and a series of chimp antics. All this again sucked in the boys and before you could say boo to a goose, he sped across the cage and again soak the nearest spectators with water. One has to do something to keep oneself amused. You soon realize their mental capacities are tremendous. I wonder, if they had guns. who would be the poacher and who would be the victim. I guess if it ever came to that, they would be the true guerillas.

Chapter 18

EXPERIENCING A COUP

How now, brown coup.

IN NINETEEN seventy-one Dr. Obote, the president of Uganda, was over-thrown in a coup led by Idi Amin, the leader of the Ugandan army. This was a big surprise as not one of us teachers on the hill felt he had the brains to pull it off so smoothly: we believed there had to be another person in the shadows pulling the strings. There may have been, possibly his second in command named Sulemon. However Amin had him shot in a manhunt which ended at the bottom of the hill on which our school was located. The coup itself was not so surprising, as it appeared, even to me that something was going to happen. Obote went to Singapore for a Commonwealth Leaders meeting and the time seemed right if a take-over was to occur. Lawrie's parents had just left on their return home from their second visit with us and had arrived in Singapore. Jimmy and I had both stopped smoking but in Jimmy's case it was short lived. Having arrived in Singapore, they discovered their flight to Australia had been changed and their itinerary was thrown out of whack. Then, on top of that, they read about the coup in Uganda. The uncertainty of the travel plans and what might be happening to us was too much and Jimmy hit the smokes and I'm sure a couple of scotches. They finally sorted out their itinerary and the Canadian Consulate in Nairobi assured them that all Canadians in Uganda were safe.

This was a good plan on the Consulates part but they in fact were totally unaware of any one's situation. Unfortunately a Canadian priest, who happened to be at the Entebbe airport, was killed when a tank lobed a shell into the building. Our situation was reasonably normal if a little scary, not knowing what might happen next. Although I had suggested to Dean MacKenzie, the other Canadian on the hill, that it might be a good idea to lay in some supplies, which he did, I didn't. Another teacher found himself in the same condition, so he and I decided we would take a chance and slip into Jinja to pick up some groceries. Unknown to us the BBC news was stating that a tank battle was going on there, which may have caused me to ask Dean to share some of his cache. Instead the two of us set off down the hill to the highway. We found the highway to be deserted, a rare situation indeed. We sped along the road totally unimpeded, reaching Jinja in very short order. We turned off the highway and sailed onto the main street, also absent of people and no sign of tanks or any tank battle, as was apparently being reported. As a result of this I am always a little skeptical when I watch the news now.

It seemed as though the street had been cleared for us and we were beginning to wonder when the red carpet was going to be rolled out. Then we spotted the jeeps with mounted machine guns situated at various intersections along the way. The joke about clearing the street for us now became a more anal sphincter contracting experience. Undaunted, we carried on to our destination, the grocery store of the Dattani brothers. We pulled up and went to the shuttered storefront and pounded on the door. A voice from inside inquired as to who was there. We announced ourselves and were told in a whispered voice to drive around the back and they would let us in the back yard. We entered the back yard and the gate was quickly closed behind us. We informed them of our reason for being there and they obliged our request. As we were selecting the items required, several trucks loaded with troops drove by heading for the area where the local administration buildings were situated. Continuing our shopping we were brought up short by the sound of small arms fire, which continued for about fifteen minutes, although it seemed like hours. This was all that happened in Jinja that day, although I am not sure what happen to the persons in the administration building. The situation having returned to an eerie calm, we made our way out of the store, loaded our supplies and drove back to the main street. Trying to appear calm, which we weren't, we drove past the jeeps with their mounted machine-guns and back to the highway. The highway was still vacant of cars and people, enabling us to put the pedal to the metal and we sped back to the security of the school. Although the fighting in Jinja was highly exaggerated that day by the BBC, as I can attest, it didn't remain that way. A few days later the troops at the Jinja barracks who were loyal to Obote, were rounded up and shot (over six hundred of them) and their bodies taken to the river and dumped. Amin and the crocodiles were the only ones that benefited from the exercise.

Fallout from the coup also came directly to our school. A group of so called army officers arrived at our school to see about having their sons enrolled. The present headmaster, YY Okoto, who had taken over for Daniel Okunga, refused to enroll them, as they were not up to the school's standards. This was a gutsy stand and he would pay for it. A few days later, around noon, some jeeps arrived containing soldiers.

As I was not at the school at the time, I do not know what happened first hand, but apparently they grabbed YY and proceed to beat him, injuring him quite badly. After this had happened some of the schoolboys who had witnessed it reported to me what had happen. My neighbor, Doug Turner, immediately loaded YY into his car and drove him to the hospital. After a few days in the hospital YY fled to Kampala and went into hiding as his life was now being threatened. Several days later Doug received a message that YY wanted to leave the country and go to Kenya. Through a messenger sequence, a pickup point was arranged and Doug and I went to Kampala to get him. Dressed as a houseboy, YY was placed in the back of Doug's old Volkswagen station wagon and, passing through several army check stops, we arrived at the boarder where he slipped into the forest and over the border

Barry Taylor, the deputy headmaster, now ran our school. It operated that way until we left in the July of that year and for several years thereafter. The following year all the Canadians were pulled out and to my knowledge no others were ever reassigned. Several years after YY had left for Kenya he returned to Uganda, with the understanding all was forgiven. Not long after that he was among the last group to be killed under the Amin regime, before Amin himself was ousted from power. Despite the turmoil in the country, school life went on much as normal. I applied to C.I.D.A. to stay until the end of the school year, which terminated at the beginning of December, but regulations are regulations and we were refused. In July of nineteen seventy-one, with sadness in our hearts and five years after arriving, we embarked on the train at Jinja station for our return to Canada. We had decided that we would fly from Nairobi rather than Entebbe so that we would have the opportunity to ride the world renowned East African Railway and especially that section through the rift valley. The story of the building of this railway entitled

"The Lunatic Express" is well worth the read and highly recommended. Rather than retrace our steps by flying west, we decided to circumnavigate the earth and come home via the orient.

East African Railways, our mode of
travel from Jinja to Nairobi.

Chapter 19

BACK TO CANADA AND CULTURE SHOCK.

Oh Canada! What happened?

O UR TRIP back to Canada was also an adventure in itself. The train wound its way down into the Rift Valley and through the towns of Nakuru and Naivasha and along the shoreline of the salt lakes, where the edges were turned pink by thousands of flamingoes. It was in this area where a great deal of the Mau Mau activity occurred prior to Kenya and the rest of East Africa being given independence. Then the train wheezed its way back up the other side of the steep valley, much like the "Little Train That Could". We then arrived in Nairobi where we spent a few last days in what must be one of the most beautiful little cities on the Dark Continent. It is a city of contrast, the African mud huts and the beautiful homes of the Europeans and now affluent Asians and Africans. Wide streets, like "Uhuru", meaning Freedom, renamed after independence in nineteen sixty-two, were lined with beautiful palm trees and bougainvillea, creating an avenue of spectacular color. The contrast between the two worlds must be seen for one to understand; otherwise the imagination only creates a partial picture. When we were there you could wander anywhere in the city without fear of molestation, from the bustling downtown to the squalor of the slums. This apparently has changed: those without will pray on those who appear to have, nothing that should be a surprise to us but often is. To round out our stay in Nairobi we spent an evening dining at the famous Norfolk Hotel. The hotel has had many famous guests, like royalty, heads of government and famous film stars. The beautiful Tudor style hotel burned down taking with it artifacts, architecture and history that can never be replaced, although a functioning facsimile has since been rebuilt.

Flamingoes around the shore of Lake Nakuru

We flew from Nairobi to Addis Ababa in Ethiopia where we only managed to get an aerial view of the hilly terrain around the area, as it was just a quick stop to pick up more passengers on our way to India. In India we arrived at New Delhi airport, a busy over crowded place much like any big airport, but with a unique atmosphere. Huge stained glass windows created a feeling you were inside a big kaleidoscope. Dragging Douglas and carrying Colin, we made our way through customs. Though hectic, the customs official's seemed very much aware of the need to make our lives a little less stressful by processing us quickly. Once out of the airport we went to the hotel that had been booked for us by a very capable travel agent in Kampala. We settled in and relaxed for the rest of the day. That evening we headed to the dining room, a very elegant place, no doubt a remnant from colonial days. Here we were met by a very distinguished Indian maitre d' who seated us at our table. Although Douglas was well behaved in public places most of the time, we couldn't be so sure about Colin. Sensing our discomfort he approached our table a little later, between his duties and began talking to Douglas and making noises and faces at Colin. He told us how well behaved they were and made us feel very comfortable. There was no doubt in our minds that his gentleman was a grandfather and knew all about children and how to make their parents feel at ease. He even snuck extra glasses of free milk to the boys.

New Delhi was designed for the white colonials. It had no main city center but lots of treed and open areas separating the hotels, and businesses scattered throughout. However, a visit to the old part of Delhi proved the exact reverse. Narrow streets teaming with people from all walks of life, from ragged beggars to women dressed in beautiful saris. Small shops selling all types of goods, hung, piled and scattered about and seeming to lack any order what-so-ever. Animals as well as scooters and even an occasional car wormed its way through this massive congestion. We viewed some historic sites and monuments. We were given the tourists quick view of a society so complex and bewildering that months and years of observation would hardly have been sufficient to get a fundamental grasp of this old and intricate civilization.

Our next day's sojourn took us south to Agra to see probably one of the most impressive buildings ever built, the Taj Mahal. This beautiful building and its accompanying gardens and pools far outstrip in reality the millions of pictures that have been taken. The ornate decorations and the workmanship are equal to any works of art, and the architecture, majestic and well balanced, left me awestruck. After our tour we stopped in a market area, just as a huge black cloud rolled in. The sky opened up with such a torrent that the streets were running like rivers in minutes. It was not drops of water; it was sheets, and as quickly as it started it stopped.

Our guide took us for tea in a gem shop and we knew, as Lawrie had been to India once before, that this was going to be a selling job. As Lawrie isn't a big fan of jewelry we were not tempted, although I am sure the product was genuine and valued correctly. We returned to New Delhi and prepared to leave the next day. I was wishing Douglas and Colin were older so they could have appreciated both Africa and this trip home. The next day we went to the airport to fly on to Thailand but we were unable to board because somehow and somewhere our health documents had gone missing. This meant a trip to the Canadian Embassy where we had to get them renewed. Although we should have had all the shots again the doctor gave us a typhoid shot and then preceded to stamp our new health books. He told us the more stamps that appear the better the authorities like it and that should enable us to take a flight the next day. In our conversation with him he told us how he enjoyed India, although he loved Canada as well

"The biggest problem with Canada is that it is too damn sterile," he said, "I can't understand why everything has to be wrapped up in stretch wrap or over packaged to the nth degree. How do they ever expect their children to develop antibodies"?

Looking at all the cases of asthma, lactose intolerance and the like, I am beginning to think he had a good point. Our kids got into everything: why, Douglas even tried and succeeded in eating monkey dung. Yet barring a few minor complaints, Douglas, Colin, and Christina, our daughter, have had no major illnesses.

The next day we were successful in boarding an aircraft for Thailand. Upon arriving we were met by a Thai tourist host, I assumed hired by the government. This young lady introduced herself, settled us into some comfortable chairs and proceeded to collect our baggage, clear us through customs, and arrange a taxi into the city. There was no charge for this but a tip was certainly in order as we had never been treated so well anywhere else in the world. The taxi driver took us to our hotel in Bangkok, again as previously arranged by our Ugandan travel agent. The service was excellent, the food delicious and the hospitality outstanding. From the hotel we arranged a tour guide who took us on a tour that was not prearranged but set up from a list of things you could do. The royal palace and the temples were a must and then a trip on the canals. Bangkok, like Venice, is a city of waterways. We started out down the main canal where the famous "floating market" is located, traveling in a long canoe like boat with an outboard motor that had a long drive shaft which protruded eight or more feet behind the boat. Anyone who saw the James Bond movie that had a scene taken at this very spot will know the boats of which I speak.

From the main inner city canals we traveled out into the country where the canals narrowed to not much more than the width of the boat. Here we traveled through rice paddies, banana groves and past massive palm trees. Now and again we would pass through a small village, where we had to slow because of children swimming in the canal, the same canal from which they obtained their drinking water and which also carried away the untreated sewage. Antibodies or no antibodies it would have killed the average westerner in short order. We did not see any nightlife as we could not arrange baby sitters on short notice, much to our loss, as the Thai dancing is extremely intricate and entertaining, or so it was reported to us by Lawrie's parents, who had also visited there on their travels. Our stay in Thailand was too short, only three days; but it whetted my appetite for more and hopefully one of these days Lawrie and I will return. Our daughter Christina did go on a school trip and saw not only the area around Bangkok but also the northern region around Chiang Mai, one of the highlights in her school life.

We left Thailand and flew to Hong Kong, over-flying Vietnam which, as the war was on, I found a little disconcerting. However all went well and we landed in Hong Kong without incident. Landing in Hong Kong is an experience in itself. The runway at the old airport was built out into the ocean and if you came in from the overland side you flew down a valley with apartments built on the hillsides. As you flew by you looked directly out at people sitting on their balconies. Then the aircraft made a sharp turn and the land suddenly disappeared so you see nothing but water on each side as you slip down the runway. There have been times when aircraft have slipped right off the end into the water.

Hong Kong at this time was still under British rule and so entering was very simple. Although the streets were very crowded, everything was orderly and well run. East Indians ran many of the small stores, to my surprise, and they had the same trading mentality that existed in Africa and India. The most noticeable thing was the low prices. I purchased two eight-millimeter cameras and my Nikon F series camera for less than a thousand dollars, the price of the Nikon alone in Canada. I also ordered suits, for which I was measured, and paid for by cheque. The fact that, once we left Hong Kong we would unlikely be back, meant they could have cashed the cheque and never sent the clothes to Canada, but in the true tradition of the eastern merchant, the clothes arrived shortly after we did and were of good quality and fit. Trust is really a wonderful thing.

In Hong Kong we did our own touring around the downtown area and waterfront of Kowloon as well as a trip to the island of Hong Kong. The harbor at that time still had the wreckage of the Queen Elizabeth lying on her side, after the fire that destroyed her. We did succumb to an over organized coach tour that took us past the Tiger Balm Gardens and up to Victoria Peak which gives you a spectacular view of the city and the harbor. The surprising thing to me was the Chinese food, it was okay but not as good as you find in Chinese restaurants here in North America.

The brief stay in Hong Kong ended all to soon and we made our way to Japan, landing at Osaka airport having first flown over typhoon somebody, which caused a flurry of activity as sick bags became the order of the day for many passengers. The orient in general, and Japan in particular emanates the feeling of an old well-organized culture. The buildings and scenery ooze with culture and tradition. A ritualistic society forms the backbone of the country and gives the people tenacity and character that exudes strength. It is a society of order and exactness. This was extremely obvious when we went on a couple of bus tours, as you were given two minutes at each location to look or take a picture, five minutes here to have a pee or take on refreshments until the next five minute break when you would need to again make the choice. So it was in this manner that we saw several Buddhas, gardens and ponds filled with large gold fish and a tour to a viewing area where we could see fabulous Mount Fuji. All were well worth seeing but such strict organization you would have been hard pressed to find in a classroom. This structured touring was totally against the type of traveling we did anywhere else. We always just took our chances with accommodation and picked up tour guides, a much more exciting and enjoyable way of doing things.

Having spent several days in Japan we flew to Hawaii and spent a glorious week relaxing on the beach doing absolutely as little as possible. We even had Don Hoe singing below our room, which for the first night definitely made us feel we were in Hawaii, but after that made us feel that the record was stuck in a Polynesian groove. Then we boarded the aircraft back to our home and native land.

Arriving in Canada was great, especially seeing all the relatives again but what I wasn't expecting was the culture shock. The changes that had occurred here in the five years we were away were really quite staggering. To those living here the changes had occurred and the transition was gradual so it was not as obvious to them but to us it was a totally new society as far as attitudes and thinking was concerned.

Chapter 20

OUR INTRODUCTION BACK TO CANADIAN LIFE

How come no one is bringing me my tea?

COMING BACK to Canada was not only a shock but prior to returning I had been applying for positions and found that teachers now seemed to be a dime a dozen. Having obtained information about some areas in Canada that may need teachers I began applying to any area with a possibility. One such application went for a teaching position in Griese Fjord, which was a small community on Ellesmere Island, situated three hundred miles south of the North Pole. Douglas thought this was a great idea when he found out there was a possibility he was going to be that close to Santa Claus. I'm not sure whether he thought being closer would mean he might get a better selection of presents or that Santa might want to lighten his load for the rest of the trip and therefore place a few more gifts in his stocking. Lawrie thought it might be interesting, a term her mother used when she wasn't sure it was a good idea. I thought it would be different after the balmy tropics but that it would mean a different wardrobe; shorts,

I didn't think would fill the bill. I understand it gets so cold that even Scotsmen wear something under the kilt. Going from African to the arctic didn't seem nearly as difficult culturally as going from thirty degrees Celsius to minus thirty degrees Celsius. However, all was to no avail as the position had been filled.

I also made an application to Old Crow in The Yukon. The information about Old Crow was always marked with an asterisk and the statement "except in Old Crow". The school day started at such a time everywhere else in The Yukon, except Old Crow. The school year started the first Tuesday after Labor Day, except in Old Crow and so it went. Again we never had to adjust as that application did not come to fruition. Rejection after rejection flooded in and I was beginning to think that having been employed by C.I.D.A. was not considered a good thing. Maybe the term "expert" made them leery. If that was their thinking I would have to agree: the last thing they needed I'm sure was another expert. I did realize the abundance of teachers and the distance from which I was applying put me at a disadvantage. Meeting with no success, I resorted to nepotism and wrote to Lloyd Deutscher, with whom I had taught in Claresholm. Lloyd had now become the superintendent of the Lac la Biche School District, in Alberta. Lloyd wrote back to say I had just missed a grade nine position but if anything else came up he would hold it for me. Well at least that was the most encouraging thing I had heard to date. My last resort was Mr. Simon Simonson, my superintendent in High River, who had now taken on the superintendent position in the County of Wetaskwin, also in Alberta. He wrote back very promptly to inform me that he had no positions available but that the neighboring County of Camrose had a position for a science teacher in the small community of Rosalind and that he had called the superintendent, Mr. Hay and asked him to hold the position and that it would be waiting for me when I returned. What a relief. Now I could plan my return without the pressure of finding a job hanging over my head.

We informed Lawrie's parents that I now had a position in this small community of Rosalind. In order for us to have a better understanding of the area in which I was going to be teaching, they drove up to Rosalind to have a look. In reporting to us they said it was a small hamlet with a grocery store, a hardware store, three churches and no bar. Not that drinking establishments were an absolute necessity in my life, but I felt it was, however, the counter balance to a strong religious influence. We also found once we arrived in the community that a drinking establishment was totally unnecessary.

Lawrie and I went to Camrose soon after we returned to Canada. I was ushered into Mr. Hay's office and I promptly introduced myself.

"I am so pleased to meet you", he said, "I was afraid you might not show up but Mr. Simonson assured me I had nothing to worry about."

With an endorsement like that I tried very hard not to give this administration anything to worry about, as I was very grateful, plus it turned out to be my most pleasant teaching assignments in Canada. After chatting briefly about my credentials and experiences in Africa Mr. Hay put in a call to the principal of the Rosalind school to ask him if we could drop out and look over the community, the possible housing and the school facility. The principal was Lou Armstrong and he indicated he would be home and pleased to meet with Lawrie and myself. Leaving the county office and Camrose, we headed east on highway seventeen.

At around the seventeen mile point we came across the small town of Bawlf and then shortly after the turn off to Rosalind. Here the highway changed to a gravel road, a sure indication that Rosalind was not a major center. The countryside was flat with many rather prosperous looking farmsteads dotted about the landscape. The area is located in a geographic zone known as parkland, which means it consists of grassland and trees, mainly aspen. Although most of the trees had been cleared, there were still small groves here and there and lines of trees down fence rows. This created a great habitat for birds and animals alike. After four or five miles, four elevators came into view, the prairie sign at that time of civilization, and then, as we entered the town, we crossed the railway tracks, which purportedly was the longest absolutely straight stretch of track in Canada and possibly North America, an interesting fact for one's storehouse of useless information. Having crossed the tracks the road forked: to the left the road became Main Street, and ahead the continuation of the Rosalind road that took you past the school and immediately out of town, not a big place. Following the directions we went up to the school, turned left then right down one of the other two streets that paralleled Main Street.

Third house down on the left we found the Armstrong residence. I went to the door and knocked. A short, stocky man answered the door and I announced who I was. His immediate reaction was a broad smile and a cheery welcome along with a command to bring the wife into the house. This done I introduced Lawrie, having left the boys in Drumheller with their grandparents. Lou introduced Thelma, his wife and Becky their daughter. We were settled in the living room and coffee and goodies were automatically served. If this was an indication of the type of persons in the community, it had friendliness going for it if not size. The family exuded a zest for life and Thelma could only be described as an unrestrained extrovert. With all the chatter the afternoon was passing and we hadn't seen our possible accommodations or the school, something we had to pry ourselves away to do.

The day was going great and then we were shown our possible living quarters. After our spacious house in Uganda, this one took on the appearance of an over grown dollhouse. It consisted of a small living/dining room, a very small kitchen, two small bedrooms and fortunately an inside bathroom. Lawrie and I looked at each other a little shaken by the size of the house, being as we had the two boys and another baby on the way. We told Lou that if that was all there was we would have to make do but did he think there might be other housing in the community we could rent that wasn't supplied by the school district, even if it meant it wouldn't be subsidized. Lou commented on the fact that he thought the house might be a little small and indicated there may be something and that he would check it out and let us know.

Our next stop was the school, a small school with a total grade one to eleven population of around two hundred and fifty students. The school itself was bright and well maintained and by the gleam on the floor, well looked after by the janitorial staff. It had a well-designed science classroom, which would be my homeroom, certainly more than I had expected. It also had a compact gymnasium that had a full size basketball court and a stage at one end. I didn't realize at the time how important this facility would become. The school itself sat on a large parcel of land. It contained baseball diamonds, a track, a field area, which was suitable for soccer or football and plenty of room for kids to play. Adjacent to the school ground was the outdoor hockey rink. I should have realized by the well keep condition of the area, that this hamlet had a solid grounding in sports. Even something I became involved in later, despite my total lack of coordination and knowledge of many sports.

Before leaving that afternoon we took a quick look around town, which we discovered consisted of three churches, two service stations, a hardware store, the community hall and a grocery store, which also contained the post office, just as the folks had said. The statement "don t blink your eyes or you will miss it", may well have applied to Rosalind but we found the other saying, "good things come in small packages", also applied in spades.

Chapter 21

SETTLING INTO ROSALIND

The country life, the boy is back.

W E MOVED to Rosalind in mid August and into a great farmhouse a mile out of town that Lou had hinted about earlier. The house was one of three located in the same farmyard and was owned by Stan Gould and his family who lived a mile north. The large old original farmhouse was next to ours and was occupied by Joyce and Duff Gould, the aunt and uncle of Stan. The third house, a small cottage, was occupied by a young newly married couple, Dennis and Virginia Van Petten . This turned out to be the greatest set up one could possibly imagine. If we needed baby sitters either Virginia or one of Stan's nine children would be available, usually Carol, the only girl, but Charlie was equally competent. For our children and us the piece-de-resistance were Gramma and Grampa Gould, as Joyce and Duff became know to us. On days when Douglas and Colin decided home was not the best place to be, which seemed to be quite often, they would sidle over to Gramma and Grampa Gould's house, where they would be treated to juice and cookies and allowed to play with the toys which, despite the fact they had been through the hands of many of Joyce and Duff's real grand children, were still better than the ones they had at home. The grass is always greener on the other side of the fence.

Joyce and Duff Gould (Gramma and Grampa) and Family 1971, the year we arrived in Rosalind

The situation couldn't have been better, a nice house, a big yard and a bigger yard still if one considers we had the run of the entire farm. The out buildings and machinery created a fantasy world in the minds of the kids. The wide open spaces could represent the old west, with buffalo, covered wagons, bands of mounted Indians and Royal Canadian Mounted Police putting the run on the bad guys. The various machines and buildings became hideouts, spaceships or any number of things the imagination could conjure up. This is where the country life surpasses that of the urban environs, as organized activities were almost unnecessary. As a result of active imaginations and self-motivation, I feel, our children developed an early understanding of self-reliance and independence.

School was only a mile away, which was great as it created a good separation between home and work and a chance for the mind to leave one world and enter another. The year started well. The classes were not large, particularly in the high school, and the students had a good work ethic and outlook on life, if a little parochial. Possibly one of the reasons was most people in the village were related one way or another and one soon realized it was a good idea not to make comments, particularly if the comments were a little critical. Luckily criticism of anyone was not a major item as the cooperation and support of the parents and the community as a whole was far above any other community in which I had lived.

Dark clouds appeared on the horizon one fall day, about six weeks into the term, when our principal, Lou Armstrong, suffered a severe coronary one afternoon in school. Our distance from the main hospital, being some twenty-seven miles away in Camrose, compounded the unfortunate situation. I clearly remember helping Murray Whitecotten, the vice principal; carry Lou to an awaiting car that was going to take him to the hospital. Although the situation was not good, Lou seemed alert and we felt all would be okay once he received medical attention. However, the one thing we hadn't counted on: him having a second seizure, and this unfortunately proved to be fatal. When we received the news it was like the whole community had been crushed with a sledgehammer. The school was devastated and little in the way of schoolwork or activities occurred for the next several days. Thelma was a brick and was the one person who gave us the strength to go on. The people encouraged and consoled one another and eventually things regained some normalcy, no need for professional help as these people understood life and death and coped with it in their stride.

Murray stepped up and assumed the role of principal, which left an administrative void. Eric Hohn, the new superintendent, as of that fall, asked me if I would consider taking the vice principal position. Having always had a god complex, according to Lawrie, I accepted.

Being asked and also being a new member to the staff, I felt was a vote of confidence as well as humbling. The rest of the staff accepted the decision, mainly because they didn't have a god complex and were not overly interested in taking on the role. The only cloud over getting the position was the sad way it came about.

My appointment as vice-principal opened up many situations then and later, which enhanced my career, more by luck than any great thought on my part. One such situation, which happened immediately, involved the fact that Rosalind's grade twelve class had been relocated to Bawlf some years earlier, a slightly larger school some eight miles away. This caused two situations: firstly, the buses bringing students to Rosalind had to arrive a half an hour earlier and then the grade twelve students had to board a bus for Bawlf. Secondly, and the more important factor, was the meshing of optional subjects for Rosalind's students with those options offered in Bawlf. This again was not a big obstacle, one that could have been overcome with better liaison between the two schools. It seemed to me, and obviously to the Rosalind community as a whole, that having grade twelve back in Rosalind would be a better situation.

Having talked to the staff, many of whom had been in Rosalind a long time or in some cases all their lives, it was obvious that there was a great deal of support for the idea. Our secretary-librarian, Doris Campbell, was extremely enthusiastic and willing to do all she could to organize support. She threw herself into it with unbridled energy and we soon had a committee organized to draw up a plan of attack. The other aspect, which helped immeasurably, was the fact our local trustee, Gord McDonald, was also very agreeable to the idea, and if it had been up to him, the situation would have never happened in the first place. However majority rules and the board at the time decided it was for the best. The committee soon got down to work to come up with a case for the reinstatement of grade twelve. Educational and community values were given top priority and with our brief prepared, we arranged a meeting with the board. We were probably fortunate in that Eric Hohn, the new superintentent, was not totally opposed to the idea, although would need convincing. The other board members may well have been swayed to our way of thinking because supporting this proposition could give them leverage on some deal for their school area later. All the schools in the County were relatively small. They probably could see the writing on the wall as far as small town schools were concerned and maybe considered the fact that a reversal here may well prolong the inevitable in their areas. To condense the story, the board went along with the idea and the following year Rosalind again became a grade one to twelve school.

The fact this happened elevated my god complex to a new high as well as increasing support for the school as a whole. It also helped me when, the next year, Murray Whitecotton decided the role of principal was not for him, even though he did his job well. Murray and his family moved on to a school in the City of Camrose, which gave him new opportunities for himself and his family that Rosalind as a village couldn't offer.

It was suggested by staff that I should apply for the principalship. I did and I was successful. Again my god complex expanded another notch. I have always enjoyed a challenge and the new set up gave me the opportunity to do some things to show that the board's decision wasn't in error and that the community's fight was the right one. Armed with a large timetable sheet and hundreds of colored paper strips, which represented a variety of classes and their allotted times, I set about restructuring the school to accommodate a grade one to twelve school. My success here greatly benefited from the solid parent and student support, as I soon learned. Having become a little more worldly from past experience and world travels, I soon realized that the rural life style, in my mind, is really so superior to urban life. The feeling of belonging and the comfort of the extended family are so necessary to the well-being and comfort of the individual. Despite the fact we were strangers to the community the cloak of comfort was extended to us with no questions asked. The satisfaction and security of feeling like you belong does everything to build your self-confidence. Thus it was in this atmosphere that I took my first crack at being a school principal.

Chapter 22

ROSALIND SCHOOL

---

*Two hundred and fifty students, you call
that a school? You damn betcha!*

Rosalind School

ALTHOUGH THE students were second to none, they
weren't perfect and one of the things I found
that needed some work was the casual act of just

dropping paper and junk food wrappers on the floor. I realized that lecturing was probably not going to do it, so I had to hit on an idea that the students would find somewhat amusing and appeal to peer pressure, a strong pressure as we all know. I ordered a number of new garbage cans and placed them every twenty feet apart or so down the hallways. I drew a two columned picture and at the top of one column was printed HIGH I.Q. On the other side was LOW I.Q. Below the first was a picture of a person throwing garbage into the can and the second a person throwing it on the floor. A picture was placed above each garbage can and I awaited results. It worked like a charm and all the garbage was collected in the containers. I am not sure this aided the janitors at first, for now they had a dozen more garbage cans to empty. However, as time went on, the number of garbage cans were reduced and the students still responded with a cleaner school.

This was one of two great ideas I had in seven years which may have given rise to the question, on which side of the sign did I belong. Being principal of Rosalind school was something like being premier of the Province of Alberta. When you have all the resources, you just can't go too far wrong and you appear to be a good captain on a good ship. The ship more or less stayed on an even keel, with a lot of credit going to a supportive and diligent staff. Having a hard working staff means very little effort was required to assist them in their duties, all they needed was support if the need arose. The parents accepted the staff members as parents in absentia when the children were at school and, although some disagreements cropped up, they were minimal.

One situation that comes to mind involved Shirley McTavish. Shirley, before starting school, was to say the least a little strong willed and was not beyond throwing a wee tantrum. Helen, her mother, a real character in her own right, approached me and said "If you don t straighten that damned kid out by Christmas I'll be into that school to raise hell".

Christmas came and went and Helen never had to come to the school for the sole purpose of raising hell, as Shirley was one of the most studious and well behaved students in the school. As years went on Lawrie and I became extremely good friends of Jim and Helen and we now laugh about the incident. In fact I was honored at Shirley's wedding to give the toast to the bride and had the opportunity of recounting the story. Laughter went through the hall, as those present all knew that Helen was a bulldog but one that when she bit always took out her dentures. Because everyone knew everyone else, the community rose like a trout to a fly when the need arose. As it was with the return of grade twelve, so it was with every other project the community took upon itself.

Another lucky coincidence was the fact that two brothers Bob and Ron Wilson, had been given scholarships and bursaries by the County of Camrose and as a result were expected to return and teach. This was the year of their return and with the gods smiling on us, the only place they could be accommodated was Rosalind. Now Bob had extensive training in music, something that had not been a large part of the curriculum in the Rosalind School. Ron, on the other hand, had received his major area in physical education, an area not lost on the sports minded population of Rosalind. Not to diminish the great contribution made by Ron's talents, it was Bob who put an indelible stamp on my years as principal. Bob was given the standard subjects of math and science in the junior high but there was a need to fill out his timetable. Such mastery in his field led us to introduce music in the high school. When it came time to fill the class, the days of Miss Farmer's music appreciation class came flooding back. Most of the takers were boys needing to pick up credits and the act of singing brought to them the same revulsion as the recorder had to me in Junior E. Bob was not one who gave up easily and was certainly a person who could maintain control. As classes started that fall Bob began his music class. The lackluster singing could only be compared to the enthusiasm the boys had for mucking out the barn at home.

Bob, undaunted, decided if they didn't want to sing then they were going to learn music history. Thus with the energy of a bull moose in rutting season, he introduced the students to the lives and music of the great composers. This was met by the class with such an overwhelming abhorrence that they begged to be allowed to try singing again. Now Bob, being a great singer himself, soon made them realize there was nothing sissified about being able to sing and although I am not a great contributor to the idea of miracles, something rather spectacular occurred. They began to like it and even love it. The class performed so well we presented the community with a musical concert. Not surprisingly it was received with massive Rosalind support and admiration for these tough farm boys whose voices had been controlled to produce a sound that, to us in our pride, could only be rivaled by the Mormon Tabernacle Choir.

A jump to the next year is necessary to gain the full impact. Now we had students clamoring to become choir members and so the whole program expanded to include a junior high choir as well. The problem now arose that we had kids who wanted to join but, like myself, were not really singers. Bob, never wanting to discourage a persons' willingness to try, took them all in and again amazed the community with the talents I'm sure they never realized their kids had. As an introduction to what happed next we must consider a side event that occurred.

These kids were never short on confidence and to raise money for various school projects they would put on bake sales and dinners. Now I didn't want to discourage them but the parents had to spend much time and effort to bring these things to fruition, so it seemed to me we needed to do something else. Something people would be willing to pay for and just sit back and enjoy. To this end I suggested we should put on a play and, to create a little confidence in the idea, I told the students I had directed several plays in the past. Now what student would question the word of the principal, even though every word was an out-and-out lie. Trustingly they bought the idea and auditions were held. I found an interesting play called, "Britches From Bond Street", a story of a mail order bride and a remittance man, set in southern Alberta. The cast was chosen, rehearsals began and with a lot of hard work and a great deal of fun we presented the play to a sold out crowd of parents and grandparents, always a guaranteed audience. Following this and flush with success, the seed of drama had been planted. The third year of the music program brought a great deal more enthusiasm and success and it was necessary for Bob to start limiting his members, so music adjudications were held and some students were cut. To try and dampen the disappointment I suggested that I would teach a drama class. Having set the stage with a lie, I started studying what should really happen in play production.

Thus our fine arts faculty grew to include drama. Some of the stars of my class (and they were all stars) were Harvey Houser, Judy Helmig, Alan Gould, Barb Yukow and Tim Buckle. Bob entered provincial music competitions and did well. The choirs gave concerts around the area and the drama group presented plays and entered local drama competitions, getting kind words from the adjudicators. The reputation of Rosalind as a fine arts centre grew to the point where we would draw people from a wide radius around. When we invited a school band from another town, in another division, to come and share the stage with our choirs, the bandleader enviously commented on the fact that there was standing room only. Apparently they would be lucky to get the parents of the band members and a few others out to any performance, though their school was located in a much larger town.

One of the many wonderful students I had in drama, was a fellow named Harvey Hauser. Harvey was a character at the best of times and so fit into different roles quite comfortably. As principal I sometimes found other work interfered with the time to create a motivated atmosphere for my classes. However, for my grade twelve-biology class, dealing with hormones and particularly adrenalin, I had a brain wave. I decide I would recruit Harvey to assist me and so I called him into my office and outlined my plan. I wanted him to proceed me down the hall, pretending he was unaware of my presence. He was then to create a scene to which I would react. He did this by pushing one of his friends into the wall, at which point I grabbed him and pushed him into the biology class. Chastising him in a very load voice and shaking him, I pushed him into a vacant desk, continuing to point my finger at him and threaten him with all kinds of dire punishments. I then went to the front of the class and asked them if their hearts where beating faster and if they were somewhat afraid, by what had just happened? "Oh yes," I said, "The scene was just an act to introduce the topic regarding the hormone adrenalin". I then excused and thanked Harvey for his great performance. The class laughed and relaxed, realizing they had been taken in. Harvey got up, walked to the door, turned, smiled and said, "I think you really enjoyed that, Mr. Peters." Then the class really broke into an uproar. However, not one student in that class ever forgot the role played by adrenalin.

One other incident that arose from a biology class, involved a long-term biology project. The students were divided into groups of two to four. They were expected to carry out some form of research, such as plant growth, how weed killers work, embryology, and such. One of the groups studied embryology and produced two small chicks at the end of their project. Two other students, Mark Loesch and Rudy Thomsen, took the chicks and decided to duplicate Pavlov's conditioning experiment, using the chickens. The boys placed food a few feet away from the birds and then with a tape-recording of an old hen clucking, encouraged the chicks toward the food. Before long the chicks were automatically moving to the area where the hen clucking was being emitted and immediately found the food. The distance was increased over time and soon these scrawny pin feathered chicks were racing over a hundred feet to reach the food supply. Eventually the food supply was taken away and only the recording was played. The birds still scurried the hundred feet to where the recorder was emitting the clucking sounds.

In June of each year the Camrose fair took place and one of the events was a chicken race. The race winner received a trip to Las Vegas, a hundred dollar cash prize and a solid gold chicken lapel pin. The racing chickens were placed in a large pen area fifty feet or more long and given a start order. The chickens leisurely made their way down the pen until some fifteen minutes or so later one would wander across the finish line. The boys decided they would enter one of the birds in the race. As they had done a good job on their project, I told them it would be worth an "A" if they won. On the day of the race the chickens were placed on the starting line. One of the boys held their scrawny entry and the other was at the finish line with the recording. The starter fired the starting gun and the chickens were off. At this same instant the other student started the recording and before you could blink an eye the race was over. The little chick scampered the distance in less than ten seconds. The boys received the prizes and the "A". The next year the rules of the chicken race were changed to forbid any electronic or other calling devices.

The hard work of staff and students to make these things a success reflected back on my administration, to which I could only say, "wonderful, glorious," and under my breath "what a lucky bugger I am." The sports teams under Ron Wilson, Doug Bowie and Ken Bradshaw's direction were also excelling locally and regionally, as well as competing in provincial competitions. These three. gentlemen led the school teams to victory after victory over towns much larger than our small village. The music program was becoming known province-wide and the school was doing well academically. Ken at this time was also my vice principal, and his administrative abilities helped immensely. (I will not elaborate further for fear of diminishing my own). Along with all this, our academic standing was above provincial average and our library, under Doris Campbell's direction was far better than that of many larger schools. Our book numbers increased to the point where we were able to send a shipment of books to my old school in Uganda. If the stars ever aligned in any one's favor, they certainly did for me in Rosalind. My mother had a saying about people having good luck, that being, "he could fall in a cesspool and come up smelling like a rose. The rose was never sweeter than it was for me in that great little village.

To indicate that nothing in the line of entertainment went on before the arrival of the choir and the drama would be misleading. One traditional event was Variety Night, an event where students and staff, sang, played musical instruments and performed brief skits. This was a great function creating a pleasant interlude in the time between Christmas and Easter. An example of entertainment which sticks in my mind, was a small skit produced by a student that involved a prop, played by another, who appeared to be just a head on a table. Apparently the head was born this way and longed to have a body. The storyteller tells how the head wished and prayed for a body and eventually one day the miracle happened. The new person was so pleased and ran outside to play. Not being aware of the dangers of the street, the person ran into the street and was hit by a bus and killed. The moral being, quit while you're ahead. The school was a focal point for community gatherings and the fun of such evenings enhanced the solidarity of the community as a whole.

After three years as my vice principal, Ken Bradshaw left to go ranching in his home town, west of Red Deer and a new vice principal was needed. As principal I liked to encourage others to aspire to my position and so Bob Wilson and Doug Bowie applied for the vacancy. This left me not wanting to promote one over the other as both had good administrative potential if somewhat different. From my point of view, I indicated either would be acceptable as a co-leader. This threw the decision-making in the lap of the superintendent and the board. The board had difficulty with the choice but came down on the side of Doug Bowie. Doug was a native of Rosalind and therefore, to take on this new roll, had to overcome things people knew about him as a youth. This had also been true with regards to coming back to teach in his hometown. The community accepted him on both counts; maybe from the point of view that the devil you know is better than the devil you don't. However Doug rose to the occasion very well and soon earned his stripes. It turned out Doug, as would have also been true of Bob, had the necessary trait of being a somewhat benevolent dictator. This trait is necessary as it enables you to show compassion when needed but also to come down hard and maintain a strong stand in other situations. I think it must have been a trait he inherited from his mother, Evalene.

Now Evalene Bowie was a determined and strong willed woman, as her younger son Bill was about to find out. When Bill's teachers sent a comment home that Bill was not working to capacity, it prompted Evalene to come to a parent-teacher interview. When she found out that Bill didn't seem to be applying himself, she brought Bill to me and asked me, if his marks didn't improve, could she have me place a desk next to his so she could monitor what he was doing. I assured her that could definitely be arranged. I might add the need never arose as Bill s marks made a substantial improvement. If every parent took that approach, our standing in student achievement would be number one in the world in all the areas of study. Doug and I didn't always agree on the best approach to things, Doug, being the diplomat, would make suggestions but if he knew the pig-headed principal's mind was firmly made up, he would go along with me and back me all the way

Strong-arm discipline wasn't necessary very often but such occasions did arise. One situation where it wouldn't have, and I pulled a coup beyond my wildest imagination, was when the boys decided they would do chin-ups on the bars over the doors of the toilet cubicles. The result was they were being bent and the doors and sides scratched by their boots. Lecturing or corporal punishment didn't seem to provide a solution, so I took action. Armed with wrenches and screwdrivers I removed the cubicles completely. Upon completion there were four shiny porcelain toilets sitting neatly in line and wide open. Now one other thing I had achieved was having students stop opening a complaint with, "it isn't fair", so I wasn't surprised when a group of boys asked to see me. Upon entering the office the spokesman, as they were all male, asked if they could discuss something with me (as if I didn't know what it was.) They asked why this dastardly deed had been done to them, although not in those words. I explained that it seem to me they didn't want cubicles as they were gradually reducing them to scrap metal. Asked if I was going to put them back, I indicated the possibility was slim. In the meantime I had the cubicles sent to the maintenance shop for repair and painting. The situation stayed this way for several weeks. Once again my toilet delegation returned. This time they had a proposal, that being they would refrain from such physical activity on the cubicles if they were to be returned. This I told them gave me a great deal of satisfaction and I felt they would be as good as their word. A few days later the maintenance crew replaced the cubicles and during the next three years while I was principal, not a scratch appeared and to my knowledge nor for a long time after my departure, when the school was then under the strong leadership of Doug Bowie. I often wished I had been smart enough to solve all the problems I had encountered and was going to encounter in such a brilliant way.

I didn't always win and one situation where this was true was in a science class I taught. A pleasant young fellow named Rick Hauser (yes he was related to Harvey), never seemed to come equipped with a pencil, which was necessary for producing science diagrams. As a result, Rick's hand would go up and when I recognized him he would say, "could I borrow a pencil as I don't got no pencil." I would inform him that if he didn't have no pencil, he in fact did have a pencil and that he should say "could I borrow a pencil as I don't have one." He would look at me in a quizzical way and repeat what I had said. This done, someone or myself would loan him a pencil. This went on a number of times throughout the year and finally Rick realized that his request was somehow worded incorrectly. On this one occasion his hand went up and he said, "Could I borrow a pencil because I don't got no pencil no how." I knew it wasn't correct but it was done with such eloquence, how could I refuse to give him a pencil?

I guess I knew Doug would be a good administrator when he was thrown a curve his first year as vice principal. Lawrie and I had bought a quarter section of land, which became a non-profitable hobby. Late in August, a week or so before school opened, I was atop a ladder which I had leaned against a power pole that gave power to the barn, our house and a shed I wished to move. I decided to climb the ladder and cut the power supply to the shed. I did turn the power off, and having just finished cutting the wires, I felt the pole lurch and then the sudden feeling of being propelled by gravity towards the ground. I don't really recall what happened next, but Colin and Chrissie, who were watching through the living room window, were bent over with laughter to see the funny antics their father was up to now. They were young. But Doug, my older son, who was out near me in the yard, realized this was no joke. He rushed over to where I lay, unconscious, with a cracked pelvis and a great gash in my arm. Doug, thinking I was dead, rushed to find Lawrie, who was some distance away picking raspberries. Both came rushing back and luckily I had regained my senses, although that is definitely not the way Lawrie considered it. I was lucky in that some of the pole's weight had been borne by a forty-five gallon gas drum, thus preventing my pelvis from being crushed and making me a paraplegic.

The incident put me in hospital for a couple of weeks and away from school for a month. This left Doug Bowie the task of opening school. Thus during my hospital stay Doug would come and we would spread out our usual large timetable sheet and hundreds of colored paper strips over my hospital bed which, as previously mentioned, represented a variety of classes and their allotted times. Although Rosalind was not a large school, it involved allotting gym and library time for grades one to twelve. Having accomplished this it was now up to Doug to implement and execute the plan. This he did and I realized if I ever stepped out of line that my shoes could easily be filled. Doug did become principal when I left, did a great job and is presently principal of Bawlf School where he is still doing a great job.

I realize I am bragging but if I don't, who would do it for me. A few years ago when visiting with Doug, he told me how much I had influenced him in the way he operated his school. It's gratifying to think that I have had some influence on possibly so many lives and, I would hope, for the best. This is one thing teachers never consider that much at the time they are in the classroom, but later in life, having been influenced by others yourself, you realize your contact with them had some small part to play in how they turned out. To my knowledge none became harden criminals or sadistic dictators. This is probably the greatest reward which few other occupations can boast, that of molding thought and personality.

The reverse is also true as many students made me feel like a worthwhile human being just by the way they treated and respected me in class. This same thing applies to communities and certainly Rosalind tops my list in this regard. From this observation I would offer this advice to parents, students and particularly administrators at the local and provincial level: try to be more understanding of the teacher, give them as much cooperation as possible, get off their backs and let them do their job. This doesn't mean we shouldn't be vigilant for the few who are not doing their job and should be turfed out, but these are very few and far between. I saw the best being brought out in teachers in Africa and Rosalind where we were respected for what we were, teachers.

After seven years in Rosalind, a business opportunity arose for me in High Level, a town located at the most northern end of Alberta. So Doug Bowie easily stepped in and things continued without a hitch, creating a large blow to my ego. The ease with which the transition took place in our school and other schools in the County of Camrose was the result of our superintendent, Eric Hohn. Eric, whom we affectionately called "the definite maybe", never made snap decisions and always weighed the pros and cons carefully. Like the decision to return grade twelve. He gave careful thought to everything and if your arguments were credible he would do everything in his power to help it come about. If he didn't think your case was sound or the "powers that be" left him no choice, he would shoot it down. Of all the people in authority over me, I would have to place him squarely at the top. So after seven years in a great location, greed overtook both Lawrie and me and we decided to become involved in a business venture in High Level.

Leaving Rosalind was hard for our whole family and especially Douglas, who made so many great friends, many of whom are still close friends to this day. Looking back I wonder how clever I was leaving a situation that was as close to perfect as one could get, as I would definitely realize during my next assignment.

Chapter 22

HIGH LEVEL A COMMUNITY OF CONTRAST

Way up north, not quite to Alaska.

"WHERE THE hell is High Level?" We were constantly asked this question. When the inquirer was told, the next question was, "why would you want to go way up there?" The reason was because, while we were in Rosalind, I was looking for a business opportunity. At first Lawrie and I thought a trailer campground would be something we could do in the summer months. However, at one point Harold Loney and I had owned a mobile home park in Devon, just out of Edmonton. When we had a chance to sell it and double our money, we did. I always had the idea a mobile home park might well be a good investment with a good manager. Having noticed one advertised in the real estate paper I decided to enquire about it. When I found out it had a hundred and eighty pads and the asking price was just short of a million dollars, I soon forgot about it. However, the agent had been talking to a group in Edmonton who had shown an interest and were looking for someone to also be a partner and be willing to manage the operation. The agent mentioned me to them and gave them my name and number. Shortly after I received a phone call form a fellow named Cecil Mah, who seemed to be the promoter in the group.

Cecil asked if I might wish to get involved and become the manager. When I told him it was a little rich for my blood, he still suggested we should meet and discuss the possibilities. Checking with Lawrie, she could see no harm in that and so I agreed to meet. We held the meeting in a very nice Chinese restaurant, which seemed to be the venue for all their business meetings. As well as Lawrie and myself, there were six others, four were Chinese and two were Caucasian. Cecil and Wally Broen, a chartered accountant, seemed to be the leaders, which the rest quite accepted. They outlined how the purchase could be achieved. As there were eight, if we agreed, each would put in twenty thousand and the rest would be financed. Lawrie and I indicated that forty thousand was not within our financial scope. Cecil seemed more concerned with the fact of management and wondered if we would still be interested if financial arrangements could be made. After a meal of the best Chinese food I had ever encountered, Cecil called Lawrie and I aside and indicated that if we needed more money he would be happy to cosign for us. This was something we had to think over and so we left agreeing to get together again soon. Lawrie and I discussed it and discussed it and finally decided to take the next step and become involved. So we met again, in yet another Chinese restaurant and over another extraordinary meal, put a plan together, as to what we would contribute, what salary would be offered and a rough job description. To cut to the chase, an offer was made and accepted, our salary established and the fact our accommodation at the mobile park residence was free of charge, including utilities, seemed like an offer we couldn't refuse. Cecil, a man for whom Lawrie and I came to hold the greatest respect and confidence, arranged our extra money. Wally was also a person with extremely high moral and ethical standards and left us with no doubt the business would be run all clear and above board. Thus, with the deal closed and our takeover planned for early July, I regretfully handed in my resignation as principal of Rosalind school. When the school year closed we busily packed our bags, rented our farm house to Bob Wilson, the music teacher, bid our many friends so long and headed north to the muskeg with three kids, two cats and our over sized great Dane.

Greed was one of the big motivators to move. It seemed logical that god (you remember my complex) could easily handle two jobs with Lawrie handling rent collections and the office work. So I made an application to the Fort Vermillion School Division for a teaching position and with the help of a great recommendation from Eric Hohn, I was given a grade eight class. A free house, utilities, a manager's salary and a teaching salary, it seemed nothing short of an avenue to wealth. And so well it may have been if Lawrie and I were better financial managers. I guess, as Lawrie's dad Jimmy was a charter accountant, I assumed she would have some financial skills. Unfortunately neither of us did and although we did okay financially, we never made the fortune for which we were hoping.

The summer went well as I prepared to set about bringing in some improvements I thought were necessary to make the mobile home park a better place for people to live. In the heat of summer the roads throughout the park were harder than any concrete but come a major rain the roads became a quagmire and one easily sank up to your ankles into the mud. This green gray sticky gumbo mud was affectionately called "loon shit", by the park residents, it stuck and built up on everything. Our school librarian, Mrs. Smith, told me how, when she came to High Level, her future husband told her to wear rubber boots. She followed his advise, but when she stepped off the bus, her boots sank into the mud and first one foot and then the other came out of the boots and she tromped into the bus station, also known as the High Level Hotel, in stocking feet. Thus were the underpinnings of this community. Many of the buildings along Main Street had sunk, making it necessary to chop away the sidewalk to make it possible to open the store's front door. Later, when new buildings were built, concrete columns were sunk into the muskeg several tens of feet to establish a solid footing. Thus the substratum was much like the social strata of the town, a little unstable.

The town was, however, a new town in comparison with most places in the province, which made a funny juxtaposition to Fort Vermillion a few miles away, which is the oldest settlement in Alberta. High Level had a lot going for it, a large farming area with flat fertile land once all the trees were cleared, vast amounts of oil exploration, a large saw mill and numerous government agencies and offices. This variety of enterprises created opportunity and brought people in from all parts of Canada to find work. This influx and outflow had an enormous affect on the school as students came and went much like the tide. Students would join classes at various times of the year which created a challenge to the teachers, but add to this the fact that they came from provinces with different curricula and standards and problems were magnified many times over. Throw into this mix, students who couldn't wait to get out of school to work in the oil patch to make big bucks and buy a new truck. These kids created problems because they didn't enjoy school, had no intention of enjoying it or taking advantage of the educational opportunities offered and therefore, were not beyond being a source of disruption and disobedience. They often showed no respect for authority and were certainly not beyond intimidating the teachers. Sister Gallagher, the grade five teacher, told me that she was afraid to walk down the hall when the junior high kids were gathered there. These were the kids I would be trying to teach. As it turned out, the group not interested in school was quite small in relation to the majority who were just normal kids.

I found the task difficult, dealing with the disinterested group, although I had a stronger link with them than they knew, for my interests in school hadn't been strong. I was more interested in farming, driving truck, ranching and doing things I felt were more "adult oriented." Its tough for kids like these because in most cases they get very little or no support at home. Again in my own case my parents thought I should be out working at fifteen, not wasting my time in school. Attach to this the fact these same kids are only average or below in intelligence and school work doesn't come easily to them, especially when this same attitude goes on grade after grade and the amount of background you have missed grows larger and larger.

In towns like High Level, where work can be found but not easily hung onto, many employees come and go and of course the kids go with them. One wee girl had been to twenty-three different schools in nine years. A teacher can try to help these kids along but it is very hard and often easier to ignore them, as they show no effort to help themselves. The answer can only be found by group teaching, where only a few students have the undivided attention of the instructor. This of course is deemed too expensive and not funded by provincial governments. However, if a study were done, I wonder how much cheaper it would be if one were to consider the cost these same people place on society in later life, in terms of welfare, prison, drug abuse and the like. I have no grand schemes to solve the situation of such students but, if money spent on so many studies that end up on the shelf were used to train and hire teachers and develop courses which would catch the interest of these students, we might end up with more productive persons in society

My grade eight class was extremely diversified, from students with good I.Q.s to the other end of the spectrum. For some reason the other end of the spectrum was usually a group of boys, older than their peers and with minds often more concerned with booze and sex. Of course they all sat at the back until I dispersed them around the room to attempt to break up the easy patterns of communication they had with each other as a cluster. Even at that they weren't beyond simply getting up and wandering back to a friend's desk for a little tete a tete. Such an act resulted in a situation that I would have reprimanded a teacher for as principal.

While the class was doing a class assignment, I was going around the room giving assistance. I had a habit of carrying a yardstick with me, more from a need to have something in my hands than as an instrument for disciplining. I am not sure what Freud would have made of it but nonetheless this was a habit I had developed. While I was assisting a student, two of the boys decided to have their tete a tete. Once they caught my attention I sent them back to their desks. Things proceeded normally again for a few minutes and then again my duo were together. This time I sent them back to their seats with a strong warning that they would be in serious trouble if this action were to continue. Obviously such warnings were not something they considered should be taken too seriously, because they hardly had time to reseat themselves before they were at it again. I consider myself to have a fair degree of patience but this apparent act of defiance was comparable to waving the red cape in front of the bull. I strode like an unfriendly giant to where the boys were standing, took the yardstick and proceeded to beat them with it until all I had left in my hand was a six-inch ruler. With this pointed stick, like a weathercock on a barn roof, I pointed the route each should take back to his desk. The silence in the room at this point made it easy for me to hear every breath of every student in and exhaled.

The room was so tense I could feel each student stiffen as I walked past. I fell back into my assisting routine but I knew there wasn't a student whose mind was totally on the task at hand. The day ended and a very subdued group left the room. That night I received a call from one of the parents to whom I explained the circumstances and assured him I would do the same again if the situation occurred. This ended the conversation, and I was not sure whether the parent got any satisfaction but I know I did. The following day as I waited for the class to settle, which happened quickly, a female student raised her hand and upon being recognized, said, " boy did you ever get mad yesterday".

I looked at her, smiled and said, "I wasn't mad. If I had been mad I would have killed them".

This little exchange broke the tension and the class returned to a degree of normalcy. My outburst did two things: it established that when I issued a final warning, consequences would follow, and it set the bounds of conduct that were acceptable. It didn't stop more discipline problems occurring, but it meant response time to instructions became considerably quicker. As time went on the two young men and I got along very well, to the point where we could stop and chat on the street if we met. As I said, it didn't stop problems totally, for later that year I had another young chap feel he could do as he wished, deciding he didn't wish to sit in his desk while I was attempting to teach one day. When I instructed him to take a seat he responded with a look of, "why the hell should I," not the type of response I took with a grin. It was the type of thing I had never experienced in any other schools. It was the type of response I would never have accepted from my own children and I wasn't going to accept it from this little smart ass. Again with my unfriendly giant gait, I reached him in half a dozen strides, grabbed him by the scruff of his neck and the seat of his pants and proceeded to run him up and down the wall. When I released him he said he was going to get his dad. I told him to go ahead or sit down, one of the two. Probably luckily for me he chose to sit down, for I met his dad later on and he was as big as me and probably more muscular, but unlike his son, he had a reasonable disposition.

These two incidents established my modus operandi, something the majority of the students obviously understood and appreciated, for it made their learning environment one in which they could operate. The other thing they liked (and I didn't find out until the year this same class graduated from high school) was my ability to choose color-coordinated attire. My color vision is impeccable, unlike so many of the male gender. I also found it difficult to understand why, if God put all these colors on Earth, they should not readily compliment one another, or why certain geometric designs, all being of a mathematic base, should likewise not go together. Lawrie would often stop me at the door and tactfully suggest that my polka dot shirt and plaid tie didn't go well together. Thus many of my better combinations never got past our front door. What happened before I got married? Nothing, because I always wore black and white or gray and white, but after we got married Lawrie suggested I should branch out into colors. I succeeded beyond her wildest expectations. This fact obviously amused the students no end wondering what weird and wonderful combination I would be wearing that day. As I mentioned, I didn't find this out until, at their graduation ceremony, they presented me with a white tie, with all their signatures written on it and an attached note saying, "This will go with anything". Although my garb may sometimes have clashed, with the exception of the few situations previously mentioned, my class and I reached a good degree of harmony.

As manager of the mobile home park, in which many students and one teacher lived, I looked forward to Halloween with the same amount of enthusiasm as I would toward having a tooth pulled without the benefit of anesthetic. To this point in my teaching career I had escaped Halloween pranks by students but under these circumstances I figured it was about time my luck ran out. The evening of our first Halloween in High Level we were deluged with all kinds of ghosts, witches, hobos and critters of every description. Our candy supply, second only to that of Cadbury's, barely held out. Its fun getting caught up in the spirit of the thing, so I usually had some disguise in which to hand out the goodies. As the evening extended into night, I kept a keen ear and sharp eye out for goblins that may be inclined to do a little destruction but none arrived. By midnight I was beyond caring and decided bed was a good place to be and I would cope with whatever in the morning.

With the arrival of the first light I was up and about and set to remove whatever articles may have been distributed around the park before heading off to school. Nothing was visible in the immediate area of the house and office, so I decided to jump in the car and have a look around other areas. Nothing! I couldn't believe it, especially considering the incidents I had had in class with the boys.

I laughed to myself. Maybe they had pulled a psychological trick on me by not playing any tricks, but not being good at psychology, I didn't get it. I didn't get it for the rest of the years I was in High Level, because no tricks of any kind were ever played on us. To this day I never understood why I was never considered fair game like so many other members of staff. I would like to think it was something to do with me but I always had a big ego. To say we were never played a trick on was not true. One Halloween, the Rosalind staff laid out all my lawn furniture in the middle of my snow-covered lawn; if you knew them you could expect almost anything from that great group of characters.

Like most classes below the grade ten level, one taught most of the subjects and therefore I had to teach the grade eight language course. This prompted Lawrie to note that they must have been hard up for language teachers. Language arts wasn't a subject that ranked among my favorites. However, I threw myself in to it with gusto. The course involved a great deal of English grammar which, with the aid of a wonderful little grammar book I had found and the practical instruction of Dr. Buxton way back in my Junior E days, I felt good about my instruction. That particular year a new textbook was introduced with a new grammar concept I had never encountered, the determiner. This seemed to be a catch-all for parts of speech like personal pronouns, prepositions and articles. As I couldn't see any reason why these groups should be clumped together, I asked others, including Lawrie who had a degree in journalism, why these were now called determiners. None could give me a reason for this new category, so I never taught it to my class. I suspect as a result they are all English grammar illiterates. It appeared to be one of those senseless changes that add nothing to the subject other than more useless jargon designed to enlighten nobody. "Educators" excel at producing meaningless verbiage designed to befog the clarity of simple concepts, a talent also exhibited by politicians and lawyers. I will relate another example of this in a later chapter.

High Level was a mixed bag as it had many things going for it that would make it a good school and several that made it a difficult school to operate. On the good side, it had a very good staff drawn from all over Canada. Many teachers were from the Maritimes as work there was difficult to obtain. This meant that many new and enthusiastic graduates had to look elsewhere and luckily for the Fort Vermilion School Division, they came there. Prior to this, in the days of teacher shortage, this same division ended up with some that were less than desirable. One story I heard was of a couple that on a Saturday morning would make their way to the liquor store in their pajamas. I'm somewhat surprised my friend Harvey didn't end up there, as I understand there were others with his type of problem. This era had created a mind-set in many parent's that their children had difficulties getting a comparable education to others in the province, and they were probably right in days past.

When I arrived in High Level the school had just taken on a new principal by the name of Hans Koenig. Hans was of German background, well educated and had the philosophy that a little discipline was not a bad thing. He was a great promoter of school sports and did a great deal to encourage student participation in these activities. The fact I got away with the two incidents I mentioned was because Hans felt that sometimes-drastic action was necessary. It had worked because I remember Sister Gallagher at the end of the year commented she no longer felt afraid to walk past the junior high classrooms. Hans had introduced some fun things into the school, like a fund raising carnival, where student were able to buy cream pies to throw at teachers. The revenge aspect of this was great. Those who ever felt they had been picked on, could reverse the tables plus raise money for the various sports teams.

There were three persons involved in administration in the school, the principal, a vice principal in charge of high school and junior high and a vice principal in charge of elementary. The second year I was there, the vice principal in charge of elementary left and Hans asked if I would take on the role. Of course I would. At the same time an opening became available in biology and chemistry in the high school and I jumped at the chance to take on that role. I enjoyed being involved in administration once more and in my new teaching role. It all dovetailed well with operating the mobile-home park, as the two positions were on the opposite end of the spectrum as well as town and, as they say, a change is as good as a rest.

Chapter 23

APOLLO

Now that's a dog.

Christina and Apollo (an adolescent,
another year and a half to grow).

WE HAD taken our harlequin Great Dane Apollo, whom we had in Rosalind as a pup, to High Level where his running room was slightly diminished from a quarter section to a large yard. He didn't seem to mind too much as they don't require a great deal of exercise.

However he did escape the confines of the yard now and again. The first time he escaped was shortly after we arrived and, before we realized it, he had headed into a residential section of town. Once we realized he was gone, I set out with the car to find him. I drove up one street and down another but he seemed to have vanished into thin air. What I didn't know at the time was he had been befriended by a young girl name Claudette Dubois who loved dogs. She had coaxed Apollo into her yard and then the house. Her parents were relaxing in their basement, escaping the summer heat. Claudette bounded in with this two hundred pound puppy and announced she had found a new pet. Apollo greeted all present, causing some minor chaos in the bargain. Claudette's parents announce she couldn't keep him and should turn him loose so he could find his way home. As she wasn't keen to let him go immediately, he spent some time with her before he was sent on his way. This was the reason I was unable to find him. An hour or so after I returned home so did Apollo. I found out about this incident as Claudette was in the other grade eight class and when she found out that Apollo belonged to me, she related the story.

Apollo soon became better known than ourselves in the town and we were known as "the people with the big dog," not because he was a nuisance but simply because of his size. He would never hurt a fly but his size made him look intimidating. I was in school when the secretary came to me and said that she had just seen the funniest thing. She had been downtown to get the school mail and had just got back in her car when Apollo headed down Main Street. She told me that as he proceeded down the street the people on the sidewalk either jumped into their cars or made a mad dash into a store. As a result of this incident, I often though I should have made a deal with the merchants to help get people into their stores.

He soon became known and Forests, who owned the hardware store, would call him in if they saw him go by and would then give Lawrie or myself a call. We would then trundle over and pick him up or, more descriptively, haul him home. After a while he realized that if he accepted the Forest's invitation, his adventure was over and so soon learned to keep trekking.

Another time we had a call from a service station across the highway.

"Hi", said the voice on the other end of the telephone. "We have your dog here, tied up to a pick-up truck. So far the truck hasn't moved but we are concerned he may drag it off the lot".

Another phone call came in one day and I answered to hear the voice on the other end say "This is Constable Beaujolais".

"Yes", I said, a little shaken and concerned some misfortune had happened.

"Nothing serious", he said, "but is your dog loose?"

"I'm not sure, but I will check". The check confirmed he had gone on a walk-about. "I guess he has", I said.

"Thank God", he said. "I thought we had a Holstein cow on Main Street".

"Thank you, officer, I'll nip right out and round him up".

It appears from the narrative that Apollo escaped his confines fairly regularly, but this was not the case as it all took place over a six-year period. When he did he could be very elusive. I had a visit from a very kind fellow, who came to tell me Apollo was being pursued by the dogcatcher. He informed me the last time he saw him he was staying just out of his adversaries reach. As it was the noon hour I again climbed into my car to search for him. Having no luck and needing to return to school I drove home to tell Lawrie, so she could take up the search. As our house came into view I could see his large Marmaduke stature sitting smugly within the confines of his territory. I had to smile to myself. What a character! And I went back to work.

As the years passed we had a new by-law officer-dogcatcher in town. She fell in love with Apollo and urged us to have him checked out for the record book, as she had no doubt he was the largest Great Dane in Canada at the time. We never did. Her feelings were summed up one day at a service station, where truckers stopped to gas up. An eighteen-wheeler was just pulling out when it came to a sudden stop. The driver jumped out and came running up to our van, having noticed Apollo as we were pulling in for fuel. He came up to my window looked in at the dog and exclaimed "Man, that is a great Great Dane"!

He was a great Great Dane and like the eighteen-wheeler his life came to a sudden stop exactly on his eighth birthday. We had left him in his favorite kennel while we made a trip to the west coast. When we returned to pick him up we found a tearful kennel keeper, who told us he had died suddenly the day before. An autopsy revealed that his gut had gone into a massive spasm, tearing the spleen open and killing him almost immediately. This condition apparently was not uncommon in large dogs with a huge chest cavity. Apollo's chest cavity was so deep if I lay on his back I could just clasps my hands on his breastbone. Man, he was a great Great Dane.

He loved to sit on your lap.

Chapter 24

HOW STUPID CAN ONE GET

Bureaucracy without reason is stupidity.

H ANS LEFT the school under conditions that I still do not really understand. A schism seemed to develop among staff members and a great deal of acrimony occurred. It became a situation where sides developed and for some reason Hans felt I was in the opposing camp. I could never convince him I wasn't. I could have possibly shown him more support I guess, but I just didn't want to be involved in what I thought, and still do, was a situation that grew way out of proportion and somehow took on a life of its own. Hans made the decision that he didn't need all this strife and moved on.

The next year we obtained a new--or should I say old--principal and a new vice-principal. Our new principal was an extremely intelligent man. He unfortunately was past his prime and was still teaching in an attempt to reach full pension. Evert had taught in Saskatchewan, Alberta and British Columbia. The unfortunate part was that Alberta was the only province that recognized the years of service in the other two. For this reason he had returned to Alberta to achieve full pension. He was not enjoying the best of health and, considering all the contributions this man had made to education, should have been placed automatically on full pension; but as we know the book must always be followed to the letter. He, himself, was a stickler for going by the book and really never let John Catt, the other vice-principal, or myself make decisions. All situations had to cross his desk: the problem was, many never made it across for one reason or another and therefore many decisions that needed to get made never got made.

In the special education program a small class had been developed to assist older students who were having difficulties with simple grammar and math. The class had built a green house, which involved measurements and language to describe what they were planning to do. It also led to the planting and growing of garden plants, which were sold. The students were expected to work out cost and profit, practical things to which they could more readily relate. The green house was build in the open-air quad area in the centre of the school, thus it was well protected from any outside interference. Located in the greenhouse was an old armchair, why I have no idea. John and I would often be in search of the principal for some decision or other but often we could not find him. We later discovered he would escape to the greenhouse and have forty winks in the old armchair. The fact he was on a high dosage of Valium may well have been the reason.

That same year the Department of Education decreed that all school jurisdictions were to develop and send out to the parents a "philosophy of education". I always thought the philosophy was to teach students hopefully meaningful material so as to advance them educationally and thus prepare them for life, something we didn't always accomplish. However, to satisfy the department's needs, we received this rather lengthy document, which I wish I had kept so that I could have reproduced it here. The one sentence, however, I will never forget stated that "education should cause a slow surge into the future". Not only didn't I understand what this meant, I was definitely unaware of what a slow surge might be. Evert was a highly intelligent man; therefore I asked him what a slow surge might be. Without hesitation he replied, "it is a man over sixty-five ejaculating". This certainly cleared it up for me as to how education was going to make giant strides forward. Had the philosophy explained education in the way Evert explained it to me, I am sure it would have made more sense to the parents for whose benefit it was produced. The philosophy contained so much jargon it was impossible to comprehend. It prompted me to write a response using much of the phraseology and wording it had used. The following is the copy of the letter I sent in reply.

Reaction to "Philosophy of Education….The Child"

I was pleased to hear we would have a philosophy of education for the Division. It was a move that was long overdue, I believe. When I read the document my eagerness died, to be replaced with sorrow for the dwindling chances for education's future success.

A philosophy of education is so important that everyone should be able to glean it's meaning and be dazzled with its intent. So why are we bogged down under such idiotic phrases as "actualized at the expense of the others…." and "unique individual with a pliant destiny". Why must we wade through empty comments like "education is a great art" Education is, in fact, a way of life. Teaching may be the "great art". Writing reports such as this so-called "philosophy" is merely a waste of time and an insult to anyone who considers him or herself an educator.

178

I resent the use of educational jargon, clichés and other meaningless verbiage, which claims to be expressing a formula for "caring" education. Every statement in this document is either meaningless or too obvious to require mention.

The over-used term "unique" is present in every educational document. No one will argue that each child is unique and "many-facetted". But to make this the central theme of an educational philosophy is hypocritical when one considers the blanket use of standardized workbooks and rigid curricula.

Unfortunately I have failed to actualize sufficient pliancy to fully comprehend the fundamental cogency of this many-facetted and unique document at this point in time.

In short, I don't understand it. Do you?

Not very respectfully submitted,

Victor F Peters, Vice –Principal
High Level Public School

Evert and the other vice-principal only lasted one year and the principalship came open once again. I was not really interested as I had more than a sufficient number of things on my plate, with teaching, the vice-principal ship and the mobile home park. However a group of teachers approached me and asked me to apply. That damn god complex surfaced again! I applied and was appointed principal. I felt confident I could improve the school, because of the energy and willingness of the staff to work together, not that the school hadn't come a long way during the past four years despite the schism that had occurred while Hans was principal.. Continuing along the lines that Hans had started, I introduced a house system where students, by being involved in extracurricular activities, completing homework assignments, showing improvement in school work, etc, could win house marks. At the end of each month the house marks were tallied up and the house (each of which was represented by a color) with the most house marks would have their color ribbon tied around the house cup for that month. This system involved teachers directly in the extra-curricular activities, either playing or officiating, as well as encouraging the students to get out and support their house. It created a little incentive, although there was still a small group on which school spirit was lost.

Having experienced the success of a variety night in Rosalind and having a similar thing in High Level, I added a unique twist, a frositval. This combined a variety night with a snow-sculpturing event. As the school was at this point kindergarten to twelve, I wanted to get all students of all ages working together. Thus groups were set up under the leadership of a teacher and the high school students, and each group was to produce a snow sculpture. To make it a fun affair we suspended schoolwork for two days to allow the kids time to work together. This worked reasonably well but again some students decided it was a holiday and treated it as such. The community also became supportive and turned out in fairly large numbers to view the progress of the work. The first year, an unidentified group of vandals decided to knock down some of the sculptures, having entered the school grounds at night. The local R.C.M.P. were keenly interested in the activity as it gave the kids something to do and so, after this episode, decided to keep an eye open. One evening one of the lady constables thought she spotted a group up to no good, so she turned her patrol car into the playground area and sped towards the group. What she wasn't aware of was that some old concrete material, now buried under the snow, had been left on one side of the playground. She unfortunately hit it with the car, causing some considerable damage. When I was talking to the sergeant later, he was scratching his head wondering how in hell he was going to explain the fact that the damage was done while protecting snowmen and the like. As the costs were met and no disciplinary action was taken, I gather he found a way.

Another event, which occurred, was dress-up day, a day when you could come to school dressed up in some fashion or other to your liking. The staff in most cases also got involved in this ridiculousness, which really helped develop the understanding that teachers weren't always stuffy disciplinarians, and disseminators of homework. I have always enjoyed the ridiculous, so I would also dress up. The first year as principal I dressed up like a Masai warrior with spear shield and loincloth. The son of the editor of the local paper was a student and often took pictures of school activities for the paper. To my surprise the next edition came out with yours truly all dressed up as mentioned and the caption underneath reading "Would you send your child to be taught by this character"? Apparently they would because the students kept coming. Although you cannot be a buddy to the students, it is fun things like this that let you get closer to the kids and feel that genuine affection you develop for them. I wonder if that is still acceptable.

As we had a number of students who had difficulties coping because of mental capabilities, absenteeism, or lack of encouragement, I sat down with the vice principal, and the elementary staff to develop a "modified grade". This meant increasing the numbers in the regular grade to thirty or thirty five but allowing one grade at each level to have a class size of only fourteen or fifteen. This allowed the teachers of the regular classes to push ahead without having to spend extra time with the students having problems. For the students having problems it meant the teacher had more time with them, plus the teacher could use more creative ways of teaching. I had trouble getting the idea accepted by the head office, as it was the period, (and I gather still is) when all students had to be treated equally, even if they couldn't cope and were not getting the assistance they needed. Teacher aids became the rage to cope with this but teacher aids were not teachers and the teacher still had to spend time developing special material. Here the teacher could specialize.

Again I was very lucky in that my teachers who volunteered for the modified group were very dedicated. All were very inventive but one however is worthy of mention as she went to the point where workman's compensation may well have had something to say. Lorraine taught the grade five modified class and one day as I was walking past her room I could hear this horrendous sound of machinery. Curious, I knocked on the door and was invited in to this beehive of activity. She had the kids building all kinds of things, like trays, birdhouses, and planters, to name a few. The object of the operation was to teach math. She had them measure, add up the dimensions, work out the areas, etc so as to determine the amount of material they would need. She supplied them with wood she had rounded up, jigsaws, handsaws, sanders, drills, chisels hammers and screwdrivers and the kids were now in the act of applying the math they had learned. They loved it and not one received a cut or lost a finger, although there would have been hell to pay if one had. It was surprising that, under these circumstances, if an injury had occurred all kinds of enquires and investigations would have ensued, yet at home many of these kids were using tools far more dangerous and most likely with no supervision. If anything had happened there it would have been an "unfortunate accident" and left at that. The biggest problem in a structured environment, like a school system, is too much stress being placed on covering one's ass.

183

Would you send
your child to be
taught by this
character?

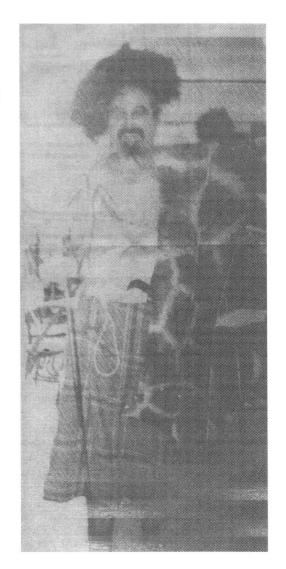

These kids did really quite well in this program and when a sixteen-person team of experts (I must be politically correct) from the Department of Education, came to the school on an evaluation project, they couldn't see why these kids needed to be in such a program, maybe because it was working. I'm not sure why they needed sixteen considering the cost of billeting and feeding them for a week. However, when it was all done they failed to see why these kids needed this different treatment. After all, they hadn't been put through a whole battery of psychological testing, therefore the program was not proper because the kids had been chosen simply because they were having problems. The other thing I failed to mention was that some kids did do well and made their way back into the main stream. I know I was biased, but too often people who are not on the front line have little concept of what can be done. If teachers are given their heads and not constantly choked down by bureaucracy it is surprising what can be achieved.

As principal I could feel the overload of bureaucratic red tape, a mushrooming of policy to cover every aspect to be sure C.Y.A. could not be found lacking and the constant suspicion that, if teachers weren't constantly supervised, they would sit on their duffs and do nothing. Most won't and some will as in any field you care to name, the thing is to clear out this deadwood and allow the others breathing room. I am a union man but unions or associations can and do make it difficult and time consuming to remove these deficient teachers.

As principal I tried to introduce and promote the type of activities that had worked in Rosalind. We already had a band program. Then a new teacher on staff, Mrs. Bozak, an extremely well qualified music teacher, introduced choral singing in the elementary section and I had hopes of moving it up into junior high. The balance between academics, sports and the fine arts seemed to be developing. To broaden the horizons of the program, we decided to take the junior high band to Grande Prairie to compete in a band festival. This was quite an undertaking as it involved traveling a distance of three hundred miles. The School Board approved the bus and funding to make the trip and parents helped with the cost of lodging the students at one of the hotels. There was great parent support and the school's activities seemed to be coming together.

The day arrived and we all piled onto the bus for this long and somewhat boring trip. I was not only involved as principal but had a personal interest as my son, Colin, was in the band, so I doubled as a chaperone. We arrived, ensconced ourselves in the hotel and went for supper at (where else do kids want to eat?) McDonalds. As the hotel had a pool, many of the kids went swimming and seemed to be having a good time. The ten o'clock curfew arrived and they were confined to their rooms. Shortly after, I received a complaint from the desk that people in the rooms below were being disturbed by a great deal of noise. This sorted out; we thought we could settle in for the night. But no. A knock came at the door and a couple of students came to inform me and the other chaperones that some of the students had brought liquor with them and were drinking in the rooms. We confiscated the liquor and I told the culprits the issue would be dealt with once we returned to High Level. Did it stop there? No! Now the culprits informed me they weren't the only ones. A whole group of kids had stashed beer and liquor in their suitcases. For me that was the last straw. I went from room to room, read the riot act, collected some more liquor and told them we would be getting back on the bus in the morning and returning to High Level without performing. The threat given, that is exactly what happened.

On returning home the investigation began as to who was actually involved and what should happen to the guilty persons. Each student and at least one of his or her parents were brought in during the questioning. It was at this point that the father of one of the accused informed me that my son was also involved. This of course was great news to my ears. Apparently Colin had stored this guy's can of beer in our fridge the night before we left. Colin had not, in defense of Colin's actions, taken part in any of the drinking. In my mind however, he was guilty by association and so he too was dragged in for questioning. Being the miserable old man I had become, I was not opposed to expulsions and suspensions. However, the superintendents considered this type of thing too severe at the time and so we hit on community service. The new elementary school had just been built and the grounds were in need of being raked and prepared for the seeding of grass.. Although I wasn't totally happy that the punishment was severe enough for the crime, I agreed but with one stipulation: that a parent had to be present to supervise the delinquent student while he or she was raking. As I had resigned my position at this time, I was not prepared to make a major issue about punishment fitting the crime. The fact the parents were involved would cause them to impress on their offspring the need for being more responsible. The fact that out of a dozen or more kids involved only the parents of three turned out to supervise, Lawrie and myself included. Obviously responsibility and appropriate action were not high on the priority list of the parents either. Thus many never did do the punishment and no action was taken. It all seemed only to reinforce inappropriate behavior. Colin did, I am proud to say, do his three weeks of raking and Lawrie managed to get some extra reading in during the process. I didn't. I was still seething inside and worked off my frustration by pointing out areas that had failed to be raked.

The whole situation caused a small sensation in the town and the local newspaper even received an anonymous letter on the topic. Although the writer also thought a more severe punishment should have been given, they chose to criticize the school publicly but wouldn't take the time to contact the school with their thoughts. Had they done so we may have had a better outcome. This prompted me to respond with the following letter.

I usually do not take the time to respond to letters to the editor where the person or persons involved are so spineless that they refuse to sign their names. It is unfortunate that such persons do little but talk behind the school's back; however when the school needs help such people can never be found to assist. As I am leaving High Level, your school will be under the leadership of another administrator, so I ask you to come forward and assist him or her to develop fair and just discipline. Believe me, it's easier said than done.

In connection with the Grande Prairie incident, I agree with "Concerned Parents" that the discipline was not harsh enough, but most parents of the children involved thought it was sufficient or even overly hard. What is fair and what is just depends very much on whether it happens to you or to someone else, and if the writer or writers of the letter have the absolute formula for discipline or fairness I would be very happy to hear it. Better still; if they would get a parent organization going to assist the school in such matters, some of these kinds of problems could be better dealt with. It may be of interest to readers to know that we have been trying to get a parent-teacher group going for the past three years, to no avail.

My most disappointing experience in the school is not with the students but with the fact that the vocal elements only seem to come out of the woodwork when things go wrong. Being a critic is the easiest thing in the world. I know, I'm an expert myself. However my one redeeming feature is that I at least sign my name to my criticisms.

Sincerely

Vic Peters

There was a second situation where a student was strapped by my vice principal because he was caught by one of the teachers cursing a blue streak, using profanity that would have made a lumberjack blush. The day of the incident I was unfortunately away attending a principals' meeting at the Divisional Office. The parent did at least come to the school and protest the punishment. I said that I thought the punishment was fitting and that I would most likely have done the same. I did add however that I thought the actions on the part of her son indicated a rather poor upbringing on her and her husband's part. This wasn't the most tactful comment I guess, but it was the way I felt about the situation. This prompted her to contact the superintendent, who was told that the matter would be taken to the Minister of Education. This was fine with me but the superintendent felt it was a little harsh to criticize their parenting. He came to see me and asked me if I would apologize to them being as I was leaving anyway. He indicated it would save him a great deal of trouble. I agreed to the request very reluctantly, but it was no longer going to be my problem after June 30. Twenty years later I still regret that decision, as I had nothing to be apologetic about.

I was now forty-seven and becoming staid in my ways, rigid one might say and not as flexible as I once was. This was because I could see teacher control being eroded away and students becoming bolder, called in educational terms "expressing themselves". When expressing themselves meant swearing at teachers, and this so called expression was hindering the teachers' ability to discipline by creating undue amounts of red tape and paper work, then in my mind we are losing it and the long-term loser is the student and education as a whole. However, as I am in the minority in believing this, I realized that frustration and dissatisfaction with my performance would set in, leading to me just sliding along and becoming the deadwood that needs to be trimmed out. I had to leave the profession and try something different. As I could never become a slider, I was only going to become angrier and more cantankerous, I called it quits I believe for the benefit of all concerned.

It was a sad day for me because I did, and still do enjoy young people immensely. I find them invigorating, their enthusiasm gives me a shot of adrenalin you need so badly as you head into old age. As I slip into my so called golden years, I would like to assure my young friends that "golden years" are another psychological fallacy that is being perpetrated on us, so that we will accept being treated like children having our diaper changed, being talked to in patronizing tones and terms and being expected to be seen and not heard, much as children were in days past. I concur with that wonderful Welsh poet Dylan Thomas, "DO NOT GO GENTLE INTO THAT SWEET NIGHT."